BenHazar, Son to a Stranger

ARON SHAI

Translated from the Hebrew by Dalia Bilu

Copyright © Aron Shai
Jerusalem 2009/5769

All rights reserved. No part of this publication may be translated, reproduced, stored in a retrieval system or transmitted, in any form or by any means, electronic, mechanical, photocopying, recording or otherwise, without express written permission from the publishers.

Typesetting and Cover Design by S. Kim Glassman

ISBN: 978-965-229-453-1

1 3 5 7 9 8 6 4 2

Gefen Publishing House, Ltd.
6 Hatzvi Street
Jerusalem 94386, Israel
972-2-538-0247
orders@gefenpublishing.com

Gefen Books
600 Broadway
Lynbrook, NY 11563, USA
1-800-477-5257
orders@gefenpublishing.com

www.gefenpublishing.com

Printed in Israel

Send for our free catalogue

In memory of
George J. Kanfer

A true friend and a genuine bibliophile

Chapter One

It was a cold, rainy day in October 1968. I was walking down Kingston Road in Oxford, from north to south, to the point where the street changes its name to Walton Street. On my right lay the neighborhood of Jericho, in the heart of which was a synagogue with a kosher kitchen attached. Observant Jewish students ate there, and so did visiting Israelis, who were attracted more by the promise of a free meal implied by the nickname of "soup kitchen" attached to the dark, steamy room than by the quality and kosher nature of the food. In the distance I could hear the muffled sound of a bus climbing Woodstock Road. The bells of St. Philip and St. James Church chimed five times.

I was holding the notes I had recently written in my home in Rutenberg Lane in Jerusalem: a summary of the important events in the life of my father. The summary, written in a kind of private code, made sense to no one but me. I had composed it on the basis of fragments of letters and notes that I had found in my father's room, among puddles of water and heaps of ash – the water sprayed by the firemen's hoses to put out the fire that had broken out in the room crammed with papers and books, and the ash the remains of everything my father had accumulated in the course of his stormy life.

"Stop flooding the room. The fire won't spread anymore," I had begged the fire chief.

And he, in inexplicable rage, scolded me: "You people, all you care about is your papers! You and that crazy woman in white! She snatched the papers from the flames and went up in smoke herself." And he went on hosing the room.

Now, in Oxford, I crossed the street in order to avoid two drunks who were sitting on the pavement, leaning against the pointed iron poles of the fence outside the seedy-looking facade of number 125. It was raining hard, but the two men, wet to the marrow of their bones, seemed too absorbed in their muttered conversation to notice, which did not prevent them, however, from swearing at the Indian lad who emerged from the Tandoori restaurant.

One of the notes I found among the charred, smudged papers suddenly came to mind.

My father wrote:

> Here I am in Jerusalem, after one great evil and anticipating another one. I am living in a poor quarter, an alien, ugly quarter. I wait. The wind whistles outside and penetrates the slats of the flimsy shutter, blustering and squalling. For a moment the papers on my table shiver. Are they about to come alive and take flight? Am I going to remain here alone?

I didn't know when he had written these words or why, but now they made me feel both close and alien to him. I stood still at the entrance to the university publishers: here, between these walls, his book had come out. The thick pillars of the facade, black with polluted air, attracted my attention, and the neoclassical building, which adjoined the rear of Radcliffe Hospital, seemed for some unexplained reason more repugnant to me with every second that passed.

My father wrote in the charred notes:

> On the eve of Rosh Hashana I met her, after a long time had passed, at the top of Ben Yehuda Street, and her eyes no longer spoke to me. She asked me again

where I was living. Again she wants to know not only my address but also what I am doing. I must be careful! I nodded to her and hurried away. For a long time I wandered the streets. In the end I found myself in Rechavia, somewhere between the Old City walls and Beth Mazmil. I reached my aunt's house.

Again and again this aunt made her appearance in the few of my father's papers that had survived the fire. It seemed that whenever some catastrophe occurred or danger threatened, the figure of the aunt popped up from somewhere or other like a fairy godmother and set solid ground beneath his feet. And her magic survived the fire too: precisely those fragments in which she was mentioned were saved.

The thought of my father now flooded me with sweet yearning. I remember one morning, when I was three or four years old, I tripped over a bump in the floor or some toy forgotten at the top of the stairs, and began rolling down like a ball, banging my head on every step until I reached the lower landing. My father came running out of the bathroom with his face covered with lather, charged down the stairs, taking them two and three at a time, and when he reached me he picked me up and kissed me over and over again without saying a word. The lather smeared over my face took the pain away as if by the wave of a magic wand. The fear too vanished without a trace and a blissful feeling of ease and relief filled my heart.

I reached Worcester College, circumvented the gloomy wall and walked on towards the railway station. For a moment I stood on the little bridge in Upper Fisher Row. At a little distance I saw two long, narrow boats on the river.

The cabin roof of the river boat nearest to me was adorned with planters full of brightly colored flowers. There was a bicycle lying on the narrow deck. I went down to the tow path next to the river, to the jetty, where the boats waited their turn to pass through the lock. The rain continued to fall in an irritating drizzle. In my pocket my clenched fist, as if turned to stone, was still gripping the encoded notes. From the flower-decorated cabin on the boat a dull noise reached my ears. I stood still and turned my head. Now I saw that the round portholes were illuminated by a pale glow, as if someone had playfully stuck round pieces of orange paper to the blank walls of the cabin. Rain water dripped from my nose and a light but pleasant shiver ran hot and cold through my body.

Who was the sailor embarking on this voyage? I wondered, but immediately rebuked myself for daring with my curious stares to intrude on the privacy of the boat owners, that privacy which is so crucial to the British way of life...

Perhaps three generations of amateur sailors were setting out here, I speculated, dimly remembering a story that my father had told me when I was a child. A grandfather, who knew every inlet in the Chittagong bay like the palm of his hand, who had served as a junior officer in the twenties; a man proud of his career who deplored the very creation of East Pakistan – one of the miserable consequences of the hasty departure of the British from India. ("If only they'd stayed a few more years, how good and peaceful their lives would be now.") His son, who had perhaps been with the forces of General Slim when the Fourteeth Army had expelled the Japanese from Imphal and Kohima, who had perhaps crossed the Irrawaddy River and been among the troops who captured Mandalay in March 1945; a son who was still too young to live nostagically in the past, but who in a few more years would probably ramble on about his experiences in his illustrious regiment and how he and his comrades-in-arms had breasted the waters of the winding Burmese river whose banks were dotted with innumerable pagodas. And the representative of the third generation – the daughter of the hero of the Burmese campaign – sailor and feminist, a member of the "Young Liberals"...

And then the door of the cabin opened with a creak and cut short my thoughts. I hurried away along the muddy path, and although I glanced back quickly over my shoulder, I was unable to see the person who had come out onto the deck. I only succeeded in hearing muffled laughter.

About his aunt my father wrote:

> I always liked visiting her apartment in Jerusalem. She was a widow. The taste of the sweetmeats she served me never changed from the first day I arrived in the country. It isn't possible, I said to myself a thousand times, that their taste has remained unchanged. I didn't know if she made them herself and I never asked her about it. I enjoyed not knowing. Here, in this apartment, nothing changed. The antique black pendulum clock went on ticking on the wall as if nothing had happened – dearly beloved people had not been slaughtered and my Ioannina was still alive. Once I scratched on the wall, behind the gramophone:
>
> > Let the clock go on turning
> > like a cogwheel in a factory,
> > The life given me as a gift
> > I'll run down to a different rhythm.
>
> The lines are still written there, but the words "run down" bothered me, and from time to time I considered changing them to "live" or "lead" but I never succeeded. Once, when I tried to scrape off the white-

wash and erase the troublesome words, I managed to get rid of two of the letters, but then my aunt came into the room and asked me what I was doing and I, half-kneeling half-crouching behind the gramophone, quickly mumbled something about a dropped key and with a somewhat exaggerated flourish displayed the key I had been using as a chisel. After that I decided that I was not the master of my fate – let the words remain on the wall, a monument to my inability to change my destiny.

These words had apparently been written by my father many years ago, for since then he had repeatedly tried to change his fate, stuggled and fallen, risen to his feet and continued with his struggle.

I was suddenly gripped by a keen curiosity: was it Aunt Sultana that he was talking about? Was it a true story? If so, perhaps I should phone Ruby and ask him to visit the apartment where she had lived until she died, and see if the lines were still written there. But I immediately drew back. During the War of Independence in Jerusalem and immediately afterwards my cousin Ruby had been like a part of myself, closer than a brother, but years had passed since then. Ruby had gone overseas and returned, and now he was a doctor and research worker at the university hospital. How could I bother him with such a trivial matter, an important man whose temples had already turned grey and whose expression was always stern? For a moment the picture of Ruby as I had seen him shortly before leaving for England rose before my eyes, his plump body encased in a white gown with the words "Dr. Robert Levy" embroidered in scarlet thread on his pocket. How could I ask this man to waste his precious time, leave the many patients waiting for him at Hadassah Hospital, and drive to the old building in Elcharizi Street to peer into a corner that had no doubt been covered by dozens of coats of paint since then, perhaps even concealed by a fitted armoire? And anyway, how could I explain the madness that had taken possession of me over the phone, in an overseas call?

I had not yet totally abandoned this plan when a new idea suddenly occurred to me: I would call Ilana Hamburger; she would understand. Or better still, I would send her a telegram: "Can you go to 9 Elcharizi Street first floor family Eliyahu first room on left northwest corner full stop. Inscription scratched on wall full stop. Send me wording full stop. Yours Benny."

I hadn't seen Ilana for three years. She used to sit next to me in Professor Talmon's lectures on the rise of nationalism in Europe in the nineteenth century, which were held in the big hall in the Mazer building on the Givat Ram campus in Jerusalem on Thursdays between eleven and one in the afternoon. One winter day, after much hesitation, when the sun suddenly burst though the wall of clouds and flooded the lecture hall, I fixed my eyes on her beautiful black ones and kept them there. She looked back at me. Then we smiled at each other. I wanted her. In a few minutes we were outside in the cool Jerusalem air. We went down to the muddy wadi between the university and the suburb of Beth Hakerem and saw an old woman with two heavy baskets in her hands. What was she doing there? There had never been a grocery shop anywhere near there, and the shortcut was known only to the young. Perhaps she was a mirage? In a youthful spirit of fun rather than out of politeness we came to her aid, took the baskets from her hands and laughing and joking we ran to the first houses of Beth Hakerem with the old woman puffing and panting behind us.

When she finally caught up with us, she showed us the way to her house, a typical house in the teachers' quarter: a single-storied stone house surrounded by a big garden. The shutters were rusty and even the thick creepers, which had held the house in a loving embrace for many a year, were now yellow and shrivelled. We went into a dark, damp passage, and she offered us tap water mixed with raspberry concentrate in cracked plastic mugs.

"Come with me," the old lady said, and we weren't sure whether she was inviting or commanding us.

We entered a large, high-ceilinged room, whose walls were lined with glass cupboards containing cases full of butterflies – her late husband's collection. Yellow, red, striped and spotted, the butterflies lay in the cold cases, and each of their hearts was pierced with a pin, whose head matched the color of its wings.

"How beautiful and how sad they are," said Ilana.

But I was already in another world. Stifled sobs threatened to burst from my heart, my eyes were damp, I couldn't see properly and a tremor ran through my body. Ilana and the old lady hurried up to me in alarm, and when I collapsed and fell into the late master of the house's armchair, they began to fuss over me. And I heard and didn't hear the old lady whisper to Ilana that her young relation, Moshe, had suffered something similar.

"He had already reached the heights of nihilistic nonconformism, and when the time came for him to return his soul to his Maker, he felt no remorse at all. What impudence!"

I didn't understand what impudence had to do with it.

"The sight of his composure drove me wild," the old lady added. "For Moshe every additional day in this world was a bonus, yes, a bonus," she said dryly.

I peeped at the two women fussing over me with ammonia, honey, eau-de-cologne and the rest of the remedies they found in the house, each of them accompanied by a story or long explanation from the old woman. And I, slumped over in the armchair, suddenly felt troubled by the spirit of its owner. "This is the land of the living dead, the living dead," I mumbled without knowing why.

Hours passed. Or so at least it seemed to me. Out of the corner of my eye I went on observing the expressions of the women conferring with each other in whispers, and I couldn't decide whether they were at a loss or in control of the unexpected situation in which they found themselves. They did not call for help or phone a doctor, and had evidently made up their minds to take care of me themselves. At this thought I lost consciousness completely.

When I came to, I saw that I was lying in my room in my students' apartment, with my friend Danny at my bedside. I never spoke to Ilana again, and when we passed each other on the paths of the Givat Ram campus she refrained from approaching me or even looking at me. And I ignored her too.

At last the rain stopped, and I continued on my way, having decided not to phone my cousin Ruby or send a telegram to Ilana Hamburger, but to wait patiently for the opportunity to see what my father had written there myself.

I walked north along the riverbank and reached the fields of Port Meadow, where I could see the wrought-iron bridge in the distance. Suddenly I felt angry with myself: I had come here to find traces of my father and I was spending most of my time daydreaming. The sun, which was hidden behind a heavy screen of clouds, began to sink. It sank slowly, as if something had gone wrong with the mechanism operating the celestial bodies. I started making for the end of Kingston

Street, to complete my circular tour of West Oxford, and as I walked across the broad pastures the flimsy soles of my shoes squashed cow and horse manure.

Not long afterwards I was outside the family hotel where I was staying. It was quiet as the grave.

In my little room I examined my papers. In one of my father's notes I read: "And after that the great war broke out." And then, suddenly remembering, I added to the sweaty pages I took out of my pocket, between the closely written lines, the numbers '48 and '49. My father had fought in the "great war," in other words the War of Independence, but I knew that although he referred to it as "great," this war had not been as traumatic for him as the World War that had preceded it.

I therefore added another line to the summary of my father's life history, and wondered if I had not been too hasty in coming here – before having found out everything it was possible to find out in Jerusalem. But now that I was here I knew I would be in no hurry to leave. I even sensed that somewhere, behind the wall of one of the houses or in the green inner court of one of the ancient colleges, I would find further links in the chain of my father's life.

For hours I leafed through the notes and tried to find a better, more scientific method of solving the mystery. And then I took all the papers in my possession and spread them over the big bed, the thick carpet, the armchairs, the chairs and even on top of the peeling brown chest of drawers. And when I no longer had any doubt that I had already read every single line that had been saved from the big fire at least twice, I fell exhausted into bed and sunk into a deep sleep.

In my dream my lips began to whisper: "Yanonima, Yanonima," and a mysterious figure wreathed in mist appeared before my eyes. The next minute I was awake. I got up, went over to the basin in the corner of the room and splashed water over my face. There was no mystery here, not even a dream. The words "Yanonima knows" appeared like a refrain, almost a mantra, in one of my father's charred notes. And I knew that Yanonima was the Japanese widow of the man who had been my father's teacher and supervisor at the university, Professor John Jamieson, and that she now lived in Five Mile Drive, in a large country house in the north of the town, where she had been living in seclusion since he died.

According to what I had heard from my father and a few of his close friends I tried to draw her portrait. R. Avior, a mysterious figure from my father's past, who had never been prepared to tell me anything explicit about the things that interested me, told me that behind the romantic story woven round the couple by gossip, there was nothing but a rather conventional match between an elderly European and a wretched Japanese woman who had not found her place in the Japanese circles where she sought acceptance, due to her lowly origins. And this was confirmed too by the Japanese students who had spoken to her – there was a strange mixture in her speech between a rural dialect and a colorless urban one. They also said that she was very proud and at the same time very submissive towards her husband.

When Professor Jamieson lost his first, beloved wife, an Englishwoman from Yorkshire, the daughter of a very wealthy man, he was depressed and withdrawn, unable to return to his normal way of life. One fine day he vanished and came back a few weeks later with the Japanese Yanonima, far younger than he was. When she arrived she knew no English at all, and at the beginning the couple shut themselves up in their house and hardly took part in the social life of the college. But in the course of time Yanonima, in her own way, became an integral part, almost a central figure, in the circle of college fellows and their wives. In these circles, it now occurred to me, my father too must have moved, for even though he was a student, his age, knowledge and experience must have granted him special status in the college. From the little he had told me about his Oxford days I learned that he had been very well integrated not only academically but also socially and politically.

Now I knew that come what may, I had to meet Yanonima. I was glad to have found a direction at last. Yanonima, I said to myself, with unreasonable optimism, would tell me what I wanted to know.

And I immediately burst out of my room, went down to Banbury Road, stopped a taxi, and rode to the north of the town. Soon I was standing at the end of a gravel drive leading to a big oak door made by a Spanish master. Only after knocking firmly on the door did I begin to feel embarrassed, but it was already too late. For the door opened at once, and standing in the doorway, looking at me with her green eyes, was Yanonima.

She was small and brown. She looked foreign to her surroundings and a little timid. There was apprehension and perhaps even hostility in her eyes. However I lost no time in introducing myself, in correct English albeit with a foreign accent.

"You should have phoned first or written," said Mrs Jamieson. (Too much makeup, I said to myself once my eyes had grown accustomed to the dim light in the entrance hall.) After that she bowed slightly and giggled nervously, and wrinkles appeared underneath her heavy layer of makeup.

I managed to mumble another word or two, and then the door slammed shut in my face, as if to finally bury my ghosts. But immediately, as if by magic, it slowly opened again, and this time without the chain. And now Yanonima stood before me in all the glory of her splendid attire. Her tiny, fragile body seemed to me to be full of power. She must be descended from some ancient north Japanese tribe, I imagined, and what would her grandfather or great-grandfather say if he could see her standing here with a lowly foreigner like me? I assumed she was getting ready to attend some formal banquet, for I knew that even in the West, Japanese women wore their traditional dress on festive occasions. In spite of the discomfort I felt in imposing on her, I stepped inside the spacious entrance hall and, taking no notice of her obvious reluctance, I said, "Please forgive me, but special circumstances have brought me here."

"I understand," she said without much conviction.

Now we were already standing in the door to the drawing room, when Yanonima came to a hesitant halt. Her little feet, on which my eyes were for some reason focused, were hidden by white woollen socks. I quickly looked away to the cushion on her back, and the loose flowing sleeves of her kimono. Uncharacteristically for me, I took careful note of every detail of her attire, marvelling at the artistry of each flower in the pattern of the silk. And thus, as if spellbound, I waited.

Yanonima stood still for a moment, but immediately shook herself, glanced at my shoes, and entered the drawing room. I quickly removed my shoes and followed her in. Suddenly I felt small, insecure and even threatened. Surely there was something humiliating in this custom of shoe removal, familiar to me from visits to mosques when I was at school in Jerusalem. Perhaps it was intended solely for the purpose of humbling people? Although in the countryside, and even in the yard, there was nothing like going barefoot to make you feel independent and free-spirited, here on the mat covering the floor of Yanonima's room, it engendered a feeling of timidity and reverence.

I sat down gingerly on the edge of a brown armchair and waited. Would Yanonima, with the rituals of her ancient culture, succeed in overcoming the surprise effect of my visit? I don't know why, but I began to think of our meeting in terms of a confrontation or battle, and I had already resigned myself to losing.

Yanonima sat on the sofa opposite me, light as a feather, her knees brushing against the low tea table made of black bamboo.

But I refused to give up. You have to save your mission from failure, I urged myself, and I decided to tell my story calmly, in an orderly, logical fashion, and then to make my request. Only thus did I have a chance of getting through to this alien woman. "Yanonima knows," "Yanonima knows," the words my father had written like a magic spell, like an invocation, kept running through my head.

"My father was a student here many years ago," I heard myself say. "He lived in Jerusalem, he was a scholar and a writer. He died in a terrible accident five months ago – his study caught fire. I know very little about his life. I was busy with my own affairs and he with his. But now I can't rest until I discover the story of his life." My eyes grew damp. "He had a secret, there was a mystery about him which always frightened me but also attracted me to him. He spoke about your late husband. Do you have anything in your possession, a document, a memory, which might help me solve the mystery?"

Yanonima's face remained inscrutable. My words did not appear to have pierced the shield of her made-up face, the armor of her so very alien mentality. But I was determined to keep trying. After all, my father had lived here for a considerable amount of time, and things of importance in his life must have happened here. And even if I didn't succeed in getting to the root of the matter, perhaps I could at least find a clue.

Yanonima had still not said a word. She lowered her eyes with a faint, enigmatic smile on her lips, and I sat looking at her, full of agitation and impatience. Then I closed my eyes while two contradictory wishes struggled in my heart: I wanted to get away from there and never come back, and at the same time I wanted to fall on this little Japanese woman and shake her violently until she gave up all her secrets. And then, while I was still struggling between these two options, she opened her mouth and said softly, "I have to go now. I'm very sorry, but I am unable to help you. Why don't you apply to the warden of the college? No doubt he will be able to supply you with the information you require."

Suddenly the telephone rang and Yanonima hurried to the entrance hall.

I stood up and positioned myself in front of Professor Jamieson's library, which contained a wealth of books in many different languages. I ran my eyes quickly over the shelves and recognized many familiar titles. This library, I said to myself, is a kind of mirror reflection of my father Jochanan's library in Rutenburg Lane. For a moment I was diverted by the strange combination: Jochanan Cohen-John Jamieson. Jochanan and John, who had known each other well, were now renewing their acquaintance in the next world and chuckling together over my desperate attempts to get something out of Yanonima.

In front of the shelves crammed with books on modern history I stopped. My eyes ran rapidly over their narrow spines: here was James Crowley's book on Japan's struggle for autonomy, here was John Boyle's book on the puppet government set up by the Japanese in China. A picture of the beautiful Madame Chiang Kai-shek appeared on the cover of the next book I took down from the shelf, together with her maiden name: Mei-ling Soong. It was a collection of speeches published in Hankow. Then I examined a series of books by Edgar Snow on China. And suddenly my heart stopped. Two copies of my father's book stood on the shelf: Jochanan Cohen, *The Japanese Empire – Its Rise and Fall*. The book that had accompanied me from childhood, the book that I knew so well, with its red and white cover – the flag of the land of the rising sun. I grabbed hold of the two volumes as if they were my own property.

Yanonima went on whispering into the receiver in Japanese, laughing and angry by turn. She had apparently forgotten all about me, or else she was deliberately ignoring my presence. And she didn't seem to remember her obligation to go out either.

In the first copy I found a dedication in my father's handwriting: "To John and Yanonima, I will always remember your help, Jochanan Cohen." The second copy was dedicated to Colonel Arthur Moy: "For your hospitality in Calcutta during the hard times. In eternal gratitude, yours, J.C."

At long last the telephone conversation came to an end. Yanonima came back into the room and looked at me with surprise mixed with resentment. Then she lowered her eyes to the books in my hands and a furious expression appeared on her face. She almost sprang at me, but immediately restrained herself and asked me politely to leave.

"I'm not leaving until you tell me about my father." The aggressive, threatening voice that emerged from my throat shocked me, but nevertheless I found myself continuing: "And you're not leaving either until you tell me everything you know about my father." To reinforce my words I slapped the book in my hands: "And who is Colonel Moy?" I shouted.

The colonel had never been mentioned in my father's papers; the firemen's hoses had presumably wiped out his memory.

There was a long silence in the room. We stood facing each other like a pair of wax dolls. Time stood still. Suddenly, as if some divine providence had softened her heart, she said, "Why don't you come to lunch tomorrow, and I'll tell you the little I know."

Without a word I left the house and walked down the avenue of trees, whose drooping branches caressed my head consolingly.

I reached the busy main street feeling pleased with myself – my satisfaction at the victory gained by my stubbornness overcame my embarrassment at my behavior. Then I rebuked myself for an optimism that might prove groundless, composed myself, and strolled towards the bus stop.

When the double-decker bus arrived I got on absentmindedly, without looking at the route number. I paid the driver and climbed the narrow steps to the upper deck. This deck is reserved for the young, I said to myself, and sat down behind a group of Asian teenagers who were busy discussing the English lesson from which they had apparently just emerged. In their broken English they scoffed at the tedious repetitions imposed on them and tried to mimic their teacher's pronunciation.

In the lobby of the hotel I made straight for the telephone. This time I didn't linger to look down the sloppily buttoned blouse of the landlady's daughter, whose ample bosom had claimed a corner of my thoughts ever since I first set foot in their establishment. "Moy, Colonel," I eagerly scanned the columns, first of the Oxford directory and then of the thick regional directory. "Moy, M, O, Y," I muttered as I turned the pages. Here it was! "Moy, Arthur, Colonel," and next to the name, an address in Beaconsfield.

The landlady's daughter watched me with a somewhat bemused expression. My behavior clearly seemed inappropriate to her, but nevertheless there was no disapproval in her look. Was she attracted to me, or was she simply tolerant by nature or education? A lot of foreigners – so she had confided to me – had passed through this hotel, which her great-grandfather had built, and she had learned not to be surprised by the behavior of the strangers who streamed into the university town. Frenchmen, Dutchmen, and worst of all, Americans, had stayed in their hotel, and apart from one untoward incident, which had occurred three years ago, when a Mongolian guest from Ulan Batur had swallowed some cleaning fluid he found on the bathroom windowsill by mistake, nothing had surprised her. Now I clearly heard the voice of her boyfriend, Brian, and while my finger dialed the colonel's number I peeped through the back window. Brian's car was parked in the yard, a gleaming black Bentley from the end of the forties, which obviously filled its owner's heart with a pride surpassing anything he felt for his girlfriend, however well endowed in the mammary department.

I dialed the last digit in the number and heard a long ring interrupted and then repeated. In my imagination I saw the elderly colonel making his way from the leather armchair next to the fireplace to the telephone stand, his moustache quivering with the effort. The ringing stopped, and on the other end of the line I heard a shrill female voice declaiming, "Colonel Moy died six years ago. The Moy family no longer lives here."

Then there was silence. I looked at my watch. Another eleven and a half hours to go before my next meeting with Yanonima. I went up to my room, lay down on the bed to rest and fell asleep in my clothes. When I woke up it was two o'clock in the morning. I remembered a dream my father had once told my mother, when I was a child of about eight, eavesdropping behind my parents' bedroom door. It crossed my mind for the first time since I had heard my father recounting it, and for a moment I wondered how the complicated details had succeeded in engraving themselves on my mind, and how I had managed to understand my father's words and expressions. But the wonder was immediately replaced by memory: the memory of how my crossed legs had grown numb from sitting motionless at the door to my parents' bedroom; the memory of the greyish door and the big stain on its side, not far from the handle, where the paint was peeling; the memory of the supreme efforts I made not to move a muscle, not to make a sound, lest I be discovered and sent to bed.

Now, in Oxford, I lay on my bed and turned from side to side. It was raining hard, the sky was lit up by flashes of lightning, and the wind blew with such force that it seemed about to tear the family hotel from its foundations. The storm returned me to the distant days of my childhood when I would wake up full of fears and call my mother, Irena.

Yanonima's slanting eyes brought me back to the here and now. I looked at my watch again. It was nearly six. At this hour tomorrow I would already know everything she was able, or willing, to tell me, I said to myself and whispered her name.

At lunchtime I sat opposite her in the dining room.

"Your father and Colonel Moy were close friends," she began, after taking a sip of soup. "Moy wrote an important biographical essay about Subhas Chandra Bose, the anti-British Indian leader who joined forces with the Japanese in the Second World War. During the war Moy served in the British intelligence in India and among other things it was his job to interrogate Japanese POWs who fought in Burma and in the Burma-Indian border areas. But in spite of his active involvement in the anti-Japanese war effort, he himself fell victim to Bose's charms. He insisted that the book he wrote about him be published in Bombay, in spite of the inferior quality of the printing and lack of prestige in being published there. He claimed that he regarded it as an honor for his book to come out in Bose's motherland, for which he had fought all his life.

"Well," she continued, like a true Englishwoman, "when your father was at the college here he would often go to visit the colonel. They became acquainted at a seminar on Asia held at the college. The colonel's house was a low Tudor house with thick wooden beams supporting the ceilings. He bought it when he was discharged from the army and invested a lot of money and care in it. The party I am about to tell you about took place there one evening in the winter of 1953. There were not many guests, and among them was a Japanese student, an amiable fellow called Fujiwara. Around the fireplace, after dinner, the conversation turned to the Indian National Army founded by Bose and Singh. This army, as you may know, consisted of entire Indian units that deserted to the Japanese from the British army after the Japanese victories in the Malaya and Singapore campaigns. When the desertions increased, Moy was appointed to investigate their causes."

I was impatient to hear the continuation of the story and it seemed to me that Yanonima was dragging it out and going into unnecessary details, but I kept quiet because I knew that she would eventually tell me everything she knew.

Lunch was a long, drawn-out affair. Today too Yanonima was heavily made up and looked as if she was afraid to move the muscles of her face lest her mask slip off. She was wearing a white blouse and a grey skirt. There were a lot of jewels around her neck. She still seemed alien and remote to me, and even though I tried, I was unable to gauge the depth of her involvement in the story she was telling. For a moment I even wondered what she thought of me, of my behavior, the expression on my face, but I immediately dismissed these speculations from my mind and concentrated on what she was saying. I paid no attention to the food placed before me either, but mechanically pushed a piece of seaweed to the edge of my plate. Though I wasn't in the least hungry, I went on chewing slowly in the hope of making the meal last long enough to learn everything I could from Yanonima.

"Moy was also charged with suggesting ways of putting a stop to the desertions," continued Yanonima. "The desertions were placing the British in a difficult situation on that front and the danger to India, the 'jewel in the crown,' was becoming more concrete from day to day. John always told me," she added with a note of longing in her voice, "that the loss of India would put the whole of the Empire at risk, and constitute a dangerous precedent regarding British interests in Africa and the Middle East."

Yanonima took a deep breath, looked down at her plate as if to avoid my eyes, and for some reason began to describe Colonel Moy's house again. "His large living room was full of ornaments. A rare collection, mainly from India and Southeast Asia. There was an exquisite Stupa standing in the middle of the room, very prominent and perhaps even a little out of place. And East Asia was represented too: ten Ming vases from the early and late periods. Each of them standing on a table of its own. It was a glorious sight, truly glorious," and the expression on her face, which she now raised slightly towards me, changed. "In one of the corners stood a jar, which I'll tell you about in a minute, and next to it an antique bellows and coal scuttle and bottles of unfamiliar drinks. No, it wasn't a jar," she changed her mind, "it was an exquisite vase, of a very unusual style. Perhaps it was its simplicity that attracted my attention. Your father, Jochanan, was talking to the colonel about his research and listening attentively to what he said. I remember that the subject of their discussion was the new trend in historiography that was gaining a lot of adherents at the time, especially in America, a trend that tried to explain our motives in attacking Pearl Harbor in a more sympathetic and sophisticated manner. Your father too had embraced this new trend."

I tensed. At last something that sounded familiar to me. The phrase "a new trend in historiography" rang a bell, although I could not pinpoint the context. Had I heard it in my childhood in connection with my father's research? Or perhaps it had appeared in one of the fragments that had survived the fire? My fingers played nervously with the tablecloth.

Yanonima fell silent and I encouraged her with a gesture to continue.

Suddenly I realized that there was another reason for my excitement. For the first time I had heard her, perhaps unconsciously, identify with what I privately called her "ancient tribe" when she said: "our motives in attacking Pearl Harbor." The very fact that I was sitting opposite someone who still supported, even by implication, the Imperial Japanese forces who had fought so fanatically and so ruthlessly in the theaters of China and the Pacific Ocean gave me a strange thrill. Suddenly a picture and a news item I had recently seen in some newspaper rose before my eyes: an old Japanese warrior, stooped but sturdy, who had been accidentally discovered in a Philippine forest, had explained with otherworldly seriousness that he had refused to obey the order to surrender ostensibly given by Emperor Hirohito – an order, he argued passionately, that the

Emperor could never have given, because the war was a "war to the end." And so for over twenty years he had gone on waging a private war against the enemies of his country whenever he came across them.

Yanonima continued.

"After a while their disagreements grew sharper. I don't remember the details, but I shall never forget your father's agitated face. Mrs. Moy was embarrassed. Despite the lateness of the hour her guests refused to leave, and instead of polite conversation they were conducting a passionate argument. In an attempt to calm the atmosphere she offered to serve tea again, even though the men had long been holding brandy glasses in their hands. But all the poor woman's attempts to put an end to the heated argument failed. Fujiwara, like your father, refused point-blank to accept the conventional Western version that blamed Japan for the outbreak of the war. He presented an impressive historical review of the period from the Manchurian Incident to the end of the war, from his point of view of course, and when John tried to correct him, your father rushed to his aid. Both John and Arthur Moy looked at your father in astonishment. As a Jew and an Israeli his attitude towards Japan, Germany's ally, was unexpected, to say the least. But he ignored their looks and sarcastic remarks about Israel, which was implicated at the time in skirmishes with the Arabs next to the Sea of Galilee, if I'm not mistaken. Nor did he react when someone tried to compare Israel to Japan of the thirties. John and I were both surprised – after all, Jochanan had fought in the war in the Middle East, hadn't he?"

For a moment Yanonima sounded unsure of her facts, and only after I nodded my head did she continue. "Mrs. Moy's second attempt to calm things down succeeded. She brought up the subject of tea again, and this time she held forth tirelessly about the different kinds of tea available, and politely but firmly silenced anyone who tried to interrupt her. She went on to describe the methods of making tea in India in comparison to those customary in East Asia, touched on the Russian samovar in passing, and returned to the concept of tea among the British working classes, where it constituted a proper meal. And when she had achieved her aim and the argument had died down, she signaled the colonel, who left the room and immediately returned with a roll of flowery wrapping paper in his hands. It was a ridiculous and pathetic sight: Colonel Moy stood there holding the roll of paper in his hand like a lowered gun.

"Mrs. Moy rose to her feet and announced: 'Now you will all be witnesses to the ceremony of the regimental changing of the guard.' The colonel, again in response to a signal from his wife, moved like a robot to the corner of the room, where the vase I mentioned previously was standing, lifted it level with his chest, and turned to address Fujiwara: 'This is the bottle of Saki I told you about. It doesn't belong here, it belongs to you; please return it to the commander of the regiment.' Everyone was surprised by the bizarre turn of events, but I knew what it was all about." There was a note of pride in Yanonima's voice. "Your father held his breath and gave me and John a questioning look. He was obviously beside himself with curiosity. But he wasn't only curious, he was also intensely romantic. He seemed to possess a rare combination of the qualities of a warrior and a lyric poet. I'll explain to you in a minute what I mean, because I can see that you're as curious as he was."

Now, for the first time since she had started speaking, she looked me straight in the eye, and I blinked in embarrassment.

"During the war Fujiwara's uncle was in charge of setting up the Indian National Army on behalf of the Tokyo Imperial

Command. He was also one of the outstanding officers on the Malayan front. The vase I mentioned was a Saki jar that had been presented to one of the Japanese units on that front, and the insignia of the unit – an ordnance battalion – was stamped on it. During the fighting, after many vicissitudes, it had come into Colonel Moy's hands and he had kept it. And now it was beginning to make its way back from England to the Japanese commander of that front by means of his nephew, who had come to study here.

"Your father was as excited as a child by this story. I had never seen him so moved. During the drive back to Oxford he wrote feverishly in his diary. After we dropped him off at his rooms not far from the college, John and I discussed the events of the evening. John said that your father reminded him of a seventeenth-century British warrior. I don't know exactly what he meant. One thing was clear: Jochanan possessed a rare combination of qualities which surprised us again and again. We came to realize that behind his academic pursuits there was an element of mystery which he was on no account prepared to disclose. John thought that Jochanan had been involved in something connected to your fight against the British over there in Palestine, which was still haunting him.

"The name of the college had been implicated more than once in undercover affairs and espionage struggles between the two power blocs, and it had cropped up recently in connection with North and South Korea and the long, drawn-out negotiations over the armistice between them which were then taking place. But it didn't occur to any of us that the Middle East and the Arab-Jewish conflict might also be involved in the life of the college. John had a sense that something very complex and shrouded in secrecy was at stake. And he stressed again that Jochanan, unlike the few other Israelis we had met here after the establishment of your state, took an unconventional view of developments in the region, and that he did not seem to get along with his compatriots in Oxford. But I didn't understand then what it was all about, and I don't pretend to understand it today."

Yanonima fell silent, and I remained seated staring at her, as if willing her to continue. And indeed she lowered her eyes again, and said as if to herself, "Your father came here by himself, and he never mentioned his wife. But he spoke of you from time to time, with pride, love and longing. We ourselves, although he was a frequent visitor to our house, refrained from asking him personal questions, and the little we knew we learned by implication."

It was already very late. For the first time since leaving Israel, I felt that I had learned something new about my father. I no longer had any doubt that Yanonima had given me a faithful account of everything she had to tell. Although my curiosity about my father and my desire to know more about him were even greater than before, I sensed that Yanonima would not be able to tell me when my father met Moy in Calcutta or how and why his book, which was dedicated to the colonel, had ended up in Professor Jamieson's library. I glanced at the bookshelves again and for some reason I whispered, "A moment before the fire." The thought came into my head: would these books and papers too be consumed by flames? And would the firemen here behave like they had in Jerusalem?

While I was waiting for the bus to take me back to my room I jotted down on a crumpled piece of paper I found in my pocket: "Father – Japan – Subhas Chandra Bose." This was something I had to get to the bottom of. When the bus came, I climbed up to the upper deck again and looked at the straight line drawn by the tops of the trees. In the suburb of Summertown two Scandinavian girls got onto the bus, Swedish or Norwegian, tall and sturdy. They sat down on the seat in front of me and conversed in enviably calm, quiet voices. I remembered Kirsten and Budil, the two girls Danny and I had met in the youth hostel in Eilat when we were on leave from the army, and with whom we had taken trips in the desert and spent two or three very enjoyable days. Afterwards I had written:

> You didn't say anything to me
> And briefly I breathed
> The smell of the sea.
> The life of a moment, only a moment
> Tall and remote as the daughters of giants.

But this dim memory only displaced my thoughts about my father for a few seconds. And then I was engulfed by them again.

At the Canterbury Street stop I got off. I stopped for a moment next to a sign saying "St. Antony's College – The Far East Centre." Had my father been here? As I walked down Winchester Road I tried to decide what my next steps should be but no clear plan came to mind and I returned to my hotel. Again I pored over the notes, the letters and the papers, and as I did so I recalled an old friend of my father's, the bursar of one of the colleges. But his name and the name of his college had slipped my mind. I lay down on the bed and tried to concentrate. Yanonima had mentioned in passing a certain major who served with Colonel Moy... Yes, the man was Major Holmes, he was the man my father had corresponded with for years. The subjects that engaged them were apparently outside the range of the academic small talk that took place around the High Table and at the sherry parties after Oxford seminars.

And so I spent the next two days trying to locate Major Holmes. In the end I discovered that he was still bursar of the one of the older and richer colleges in Oxford. In a brief telephone conversation the man, who sounded genial and friendly, confirmed that he had known my father and invited me to come and see him in his office.

"Major Holmes will see you at once," his secretary informed me, and a few minutes later the major came into the room and shook me warmly by the hand. With interest and even curiosity he looked me over from top to toe. An impressive figure of a man, he seemed perfectly in tune with the rich furnishings of his domain in the college. He was about sixty-five years old, and boasted a grey moustache, a head of thick black hair going grey at the temples, and a pin-striped blue suit.

For a moment it seemed to me that the figure standing before me had stepped out of one of the heavy frames surrounding the dark portraits of the elders and dignitaries of the college, which had accumulated on the walls during the long years of its existence and which had accompanied me from the moment I entered the building. Only his red tie seemed a little loud and inappropriate to the figure I had imagined before I came. Could it be that behind the imposing, formal facade lurked a mischievous, unconventional personality? This impression was reinforced when I looked into his eyes, which twinkled with the laughter of a man who took the rules of whatever game he happened to be playing with a certain measure of light-heartedness and amused skepticism. The major settled himself behind his desk and motioned me to the capacious leather armchair in the corner. I noticed that he dragged his right leg slightly when he walked, and this gave rise to a new series of questions in my mind.

"I heard from Mrs. Jamieson about your tragedy," he said. "I had no idea, but I wondered why I hadn't heard from John lately. Please accept my condolences."

"Thank you," I said. "I know that you were close friends."

"Your father was a fine man. We had a great deal in common," he said without elaborating.

"If I'm not mistaken, you served with Colonel Moy in India," I said and immediately regretted my directness.

"Yes, we tried to prevent massive desertions to Bose's army, but we failed," replied Holmes shortly.

He seemed displeased by the turn the conversation had taken. But there was no trace of regret for the British failure in his voice. His expression was one of indifference and even disdain. Was this due only to the remoteness of the events in question, or had Holmes too, like Colonel Moy, been seduced by the Indian National Army? And perhaps it was this that had brought my father so close to the major? All this was idle speculation, since I still didn't know what my father had done in the war, and what had taken him to a place so remote from Palestine and the threat of the German troops advancing in North Africa; and how had he been affected later by the news of the extent of the holocaust of European Jewry?

I knew about the attempts of Lechi ("Fighters for the Freedom of Israel"), the radical paramilitary anti-British Jewish underground in Mandatory Palestine, otherwise known as the Stern Gang, to contact representatives of fascist Italy and Nazi Germany in 1941. I even remembered how upset I had been when I first read about it in a newspaper article after the war, and how my father had tried to soften my indignation when we strolled together down Ben-Maimon Boulevard one cool Jerusalem evening. But all this only deepened the mystery. Why, I cursed myself, had I left it so late? Why hadn't I tackled my father about it when I had the chance? Was father a formal member of Lechi? Was it possible that someone had also tried to enter into negotiations with the militaristic Tojo regime in Japan?

The conversation with Major Holmes proceeded at a leisurely pace. Apart from the mention, almost in passing, of someone called George Woodhead who had served in British intelligence in the Far East during the war and who was still living in Hong Kong, nothing of any significance was said. Suddenly, like a navigator extricating his ship from a dangerous reef and breaking into the open sea, I stopped beating about the bush and said, "Will you please tell me, Major Holmes, what my father, a Jew from Palestine, was doing with your people at the other end of the world, in Chittagong Bay, in Kohima and Imphal? I'd like an explanation. That's what I came to see you for, after all." And I added impatiently: "I think you're hiding something from me."

Major Holmes trembled and his cheeks flushed. He rose to his feet and said sharply, "Please control yourself, Mr. Cohen. I never saw your father lose his temper, and believe me, I knew him well. He was a gentleman, and my good friend. I have nothing more to say to you. You can see yourself out." He turned on his heel and left the room.

The door to the past, I said bitterly to myself as I sat in a pub across the street and sipped a beer, will apparently remain locked to me. My anger against myself grew: why hadn't I waited patiently for the right moment, why hadn't I been more calculating and sophisticated in my questioning of the major, instead of bursting out like that? But I was angry with Holmes too: if he was really such a good friend of my father's, why had he treated me like that and refused to answer the question that was troubling me so deeply?

After I had calmed down and taken a stroll though the shopping center, I came to the vague and unfounded conclusion that my father had been connected in some way to a pro-Japanese group during the Second World War. I knew that many of the exploits of the underground movements in Palestine had not been properly investigated, not even those that had ostensibly been made public, because the people involved in the "activist groups" were either unable or unwilling to reveal all their secrets.

To myself I called them "activist groups" and not by the explicit name of Lechi or the Stern Gang, because I felt that my father, even though he had been connected to Lechi, did not represent the mainstream of this organization. It was even difficult for me to define his views along the conventional lines of "right" and "left." My father was too original and too much of an individualist to be pigeonholed in this way. Perhaps my father was even more extreme and even less clear politically than Yair (the underground name of Avraham Stern, head of the "Stern Gang") himself – so much so, indeed, that it was impossible to know exactly what lay behind his anti-imperialist activities and how he saw the political, social and economic picture at the end of the global conflict. Like Yair, my father was a man whose intellectual curiosity added a special dimension to his personality without helping to clarify his political position. On the contrary, it seemed to me that both men were characterized by a basic naivety. During the period of the struggle itself this may have been a good thing, but afterwards? Yair was removed from the stage in the middle of the war by CID Officer Geoffrey Morton's shots, but my father lived another twenty-six years... Did he take stock of his positions and opinions with regard to issues that came up every day? What was his attitude to the kibbutz movement, to Ben Gurion, to Begin, to the Arab-Israeli conflict? Whom did he vote for in the elections after the establishment of the State of Israel?

Again I reviewed his small circle of friends. I had never had a frank conversation with any of them, I knew nothing of their political or even their family backgrounds. I overheard references to the activities of this or that "uncle" as a child, but I understood nothing. Did I know, for instance, the real name of R. Avior, apparently one of my father's severest critics during the struggle against the British? Who exactly was Spielberg, whose name was always mentioned with bated breath and whose sayings were quoted with almost religious awe? The more I considered these disturbing questions, the more it dawned on me that the men who had stroked my head as a child avoided my questions and shrank from my curiosity as I grew older. And today Major Holmes, too, had joined my father's "circle of friends."

At this point in my reflections I reached the Ashmolean library at the top of St. Giles, Oxford's main street.

Chapter Two

Two years after her husband Shlomo died, in 1966, Sarina arrived unexpectedly in Hong Kong. From the veranda of her spacious home on the island, high up on the hill, she would look down on the busy port and the dozens of ships sailing in the bay or setting out for distant lands. Her past now seemed remote to her: the comfortable house in Ioannina in northern Greece, her daughters, Bracha and Adina, and the Jewish quarter whose streets, people and atmosphere were as familiar to her as the palm of her hand.

Shlomo had died suddenly. No, she corrected herself, he had taken months and years to die, and she had nursed him until his soul departed his body with a rattle she would never forget. Bracha, the eldest daughter, did everything with quick movements, as if driven by invisible forces, and her restlessness infected everyone around her. With her skinny, fragile body she resembled her dead father when he was borne to his grave to the sound of the professional mourners. Many professional mourners had gathered outside their house that day, perhaps because the deceased was reputed to be a wealthy, prominent man, even though he was actually only a merchant of moderate means who earned a respectable living from the textile shop he had inherited from his father.

As for the younger daughter, Adina, she was in love. She spent much of her time supine on a wicker sofa that threatened to collapse beneath the weight of her plump body, which always smelled faintly of sweat. Sarina had tried again and again to get rid of this "disgraceful" piece of furniture, but her husband objected. "When I go you can do as you please," he would groan. And now he had gone.

She fulfilled all her obligations to him, according to all the rules and rituals of tradition, but the sofa she threw out even before she had taken off her mourning clothes. Then she spring-cleaned the house, gave the dead man's clothes to relatives and neighbors, had his photograph enlarged by Atias the photographer, and stood it on the wooden chest in the bedroom.

For many months she wore black. She was a beautiful woman; her figure was shapely, her breasts were still full and her hair fell in waves to her shoulders. They had been married for thirty-two years.

Now she sat on her veranda in this strange, foreign colony. Her eye fell on the skyscraper to her left, somewhere down in the commercial center. How small it seemed from up here, and how tall and impressive it had looked when she stood next to it on her morning shopping expeditions accompanied by her faithful driver. From the skyscraper her glance shifted to the blue bay. And immediately, mechanically, she turned her head towards the big living room whose great glass doors opened onto the veranda, and for a long time her eyes rested on the cupboard of stuffed birds so dear to the heart of her patron, Leonardo Reil. He devoted most of his leisure time to this hobby of his. When he returned from his business affairs in the center of town, he would run his fingers through her hair while his eyes caressed the birds in the black cupboard. The Chinese "boy" dusted the cupboard every day just before his master came home.

Leonardo's active social life filled Sarina's heart with fears of her own inadequacy. Although in her previous life, in Ioannina, she had been considered a woman of the world and well known for her intelligence and resourcefulness, here in the colony she would stand about at social functions like a beautiful but somewhat old-fashioned article of furniture, a lifeless ornament.

The sentences she pronounced in a faint voice, in English or French, fell on the air without making any impression or giving rise to any reaction. And she would stand there with her eyes darting round the room like the eyes of a trapped animal. And but for Leonardo the tears choking her throat would have welled up again and again and flooded her eyes. But he never took his eyes off her, and from time to time he would cut short his conversation with his associates, and lead her gently to a secluded corner, where he would encourage her and ply her with drinks until she recovered her composure.

On Christmas and on a few other occasions they would go to church – a dark, heavy building erected at the beginning of the century by the British business community permanently settled in the colony. Leonardo and Sarina had reserved seats in the center of the hall. She would sit there, and to the sonorous strains of the organ she would examine the crucified figure of Christ with a forgiving expression on her face, glancing occasionally at the Virgin Mary with her golden halo. Although she had only attended the synagogue in Ioannina regularly in her childhood, after her marriage the Sabbaths and Holy Days had become a part of her being and way of life. On Thursday she would cook for the Sabbath, on Friday the floors were washed and the house was spotlessly clean, and on Saturday morning, when her husband Shlomo went to the synagogue, she would listen secretly to Greek music on the radio, take care of her complexion, and make up her eyes. Rosh Hashana, Yom Kippur, Sukkoth, Passover and Shavuoth were scrupulously observed both in her parents' house and in her own home. And as they sat in the church she would remember all these things, until Leonardo, who seemed to guess her thoughts, would sometimes have to remind her that the service was over and it was time for them to go home.

The firm of "Leonardo Reil Co. Ltd. – Textile and Household Goods, Import and Export" – was well known in the Far East. And since Leonardo had no sons, he had taken two intelligent Chinese employees from his head office in Hong Kong and made them privy to his business secrets. A few months before he left for Greece – where he would meet Sarina – he transferred one percent of the shares each to his two faithful assistants and changed the name of the firm to "Leonardo Reil and Partners, Co. Ltd." This step gave him great satisfaction and even a certain paternal feeling. He sailed to Greece because his doctors had ordered a holiday from work, a relaxation of tension, and a change of climate and atmosphere – or else, they threatened, he would come to a bad end.

At the port of Piraeus (after three weeks at sea on the passenger ship which had sailed around the Cape of Good Hope) Leonardo was met by a car with a driver which took him straight to Salonika. Northern Greece seemed more attractive to him than the tourist-thronged Athens. And there, in a clean, pleasant hotel, he spent his days reading, thinking, and swimming in the clear pool. In the evenings he strolled leisurely along the harbor road and enjoyed the sea breeze ruffling his sparse hair. On the tenth day of his stay he was already tired of resting and thinking and sick of reading.

The next day he set out in a hired car on the narrow winding road that led from Salonika to the west. He drove fast, too fast for his age and the condition of his health. On more than one occasion he was forced onto the shoulder by a truck loaded with agricultural produce coming up opposite him and blocking the road. But he felt no fear. When hope is lost, he said to himself, so is fear. His state of mind was due not to any sense of failure, but rather to his great success and the feeling that his life had reached a dead end because he had no one with whom to share the fruits of this success: he had not married and produced children, nor did he have any close relatives. One bitter thought gave him no rest: if I die on this godforsaken road, all I own will go to my two assistants, and what belonged to the Chinese in the first place will return to them.

The sun was about to sink, and in the twilight, after another dangerous curve which he turned with a screeching of brakes, he found himself face-to-face with a fairytale town built on the banks of a glorious lake, with an ancient castle and little houses scattered over a hill and clustering at its feet. With his heart pounding he drove slowly into the town – Ioannina.

Leonardo was the only son of parents who died young, and as soon as he came of age he began to wander the world. About his family he knew very little, and he had never taken the trouble to find out anything more. He spent the years engaging in international commerce, and like the goods he dealt in so too he changed his homes and friends again and again, without ever forming any deep attachments. After the war he settled in cosmopolitan and colorful Hong Kong, and it became his home. Now, in Ioannina, he was engulfed by an emotion he had not felt for years, but he knew that it was not Greece, nor this town hidden in its north, which had given rise to it. At the same time he knew with a clear and certain conviction that the time had come for him to settle down and put out roots.

After eating his fill at the tiny hotel where he took a room, he went out to walk around the town. On the broad promenade he encountered people strolling with their families in a kind of tranquility that he had never come across before. Dark-haired little girls peeped at mischievous boys and stifled shy giggles. Outside cafés and restaurants tables were dotted over the wide pavements. Mauve neon lights and huge revolving fans created an atmosphere of restfulness after the day's work. He turned into a steep, narrow street climbing up the hillside, and strayed pleasurably in dim, narrow alleys between clean, sleepy courtyards. Suddenly he stopped next to one of the houses, which was surrounded by a little garden overgrown with weeds. There was a little pool in the middle of the garden, and the light from a large, low window was reflected in it.

She sat next to the window, straight-backed and dressed in black. For a moment she took off her glasses and looked at him. He roused himself and moved a few steps away, but immediately hurried back again, as if bewitched. She stood up and came closer to the window. As in a dream he heard her clear, tender voice. Was she asking him something? Then she vanished from the window and reappeared immediately on the gravel path in the garden, opened the gate, which he had not noticed before, and stood still. Now they stood facing each other. He felt a powerful surge of emotion, unlike anything he had felt for years. She came out, closed the gate behind her, and said in English with a faint Greek accent, "I'll show you the way."

She stepped lightly, the tapping of her heels breaking the silence of the little cobbled street. And he matched his steps to hers.

For eight days Leonardo Reil stayed in Ioannina. Like bosom friends meeting again after spending years apart, they delighted in each other's company. On the ninth day she packed a few of her possessions and was ready to leave.

Sarina had already been living in Hong Kong for a year. And one fine Monday afternoon the sky grew prematurely dark. The Chinese boy had already dusted the cupboard holding the stuffed birds, but Leonardo did not come. She waited and waited, pacing to and fro in the spacious living room, but still he did not come. The boy gave her a puzzled look, and then, alarmed by his own boldness, he said in broken English, "Why master not here Chiang not know."

Evening fell and supper replaced the lunch which had turned cold on the table.

"Where are you, Leonardo?" Sarina cried aloud.

But when the boy heard her cry and came running into the room, she sent him away. Suddenly a strange calm descended on her, she phoned for a cab, and for the first time since her arrival in the colony she went out alone to the "Leonardo Reil" offices in Queen Street.

The center of town was swarming with police and militia. Helicopters hovered overhead. The streets were blocked by standing traffic and throngs of Chinese. The whole area was in a turmoil. Sarina got out of the taxi, hurried into a side alley, went through a narrow passage, and after crossing two streets found herself not far from the entrance to the building housing her husband's firm. Gangs of excited youths barred her way. They were angry and uncharacteristically unruly. Chinese policemen and their British officers ran to and fro.

"This uprising is the end of us here," said one of the officers – a tall Englishman – and his moustache trembled in a nervous spasm.

"Red Guards, Cultural Revolution, God knows what else is in store for us here. It looks as if old Mao has really taken leave of his senses. He won't be able to return this genie to the bottle," grumbled a sergeant-major whose decorations proclaimed him to be a veteran of the war in Malaya.

Little by little, with stubborn determination, Sarina pushed her way to the building entrance until she stood trembling, her hair dishevelled and the top button of her blouse undone, in front of the familiar iron gate where her benefactor's name was emblazoned in English and Chinese. The gate was shut, not with the usual lock and bolt, but with iron chains which looked as if someone had hastily fastened them there from inside. On the other side of the bars, in the courtyard, she could see a number of the employees, their elegant suits slightly rumpled, standing silently with iron bars, belts and stones in their hands, and expressions of bewilderment on their faces, as if they were wondering how they had gotten into this unexpected situation. In spite of the gleam of victory in their eyes they were unable to hide their fear at what they had done.

Sarina fell on the gate, first pleadingly and then furiously.

"*Revuelta, revuelta!* (Revolt, revolt!)" she heard herself muttering in Ladino.

With a force that took her by surprise she pounded on the chain with a heavy stone she found at her feet. The Chinese youths stared at the European woman in astonishment, not daring to say a word or raise a finger. Feeling as if something inside her had shifted irrevocably and she would never be the same again, she removed the chain after breaking one of the links, kicked the heavy gate which opened with a discordant creak, and burst into the courtyard. On the left, in a corner hitherto hidden from her eyes, she saw Leonardo sitting on the stone floor, bound hand and foot, his head hanging and dark, thick blood streaming from his nose. When he saw Sarina kneeling by his side he raised his head painfully and smiled a sad smile.

"The Reds," he whispered, "look what they've done to me. Let's escape to the mountains, my lovely girl, to the fields."

At the sound of this romantic phrase, so out of place in the circumstances (the last time she had heard these words was in Ioannina, when he was persuading her to come with him), she too smiled.

Now she saw Leonardo's two assistants. With lowered eyes, they stood mutely in a corner of the courtyard without daring to move from their places. The other employees had vanished. She freed Leonardo from his fetters, and he stood up, dusted off his trousers, took a handkerchief out of his pocket, and gently wiped the congealed blood from his nose. They walked out of the gate together without anyone trying to stop them.

In the coming days and weeks order was ostensibly restored. Both the British and the Chinese in Hong Kong realized that the authorities in Peking were not interested in widening the rift with the colony, and would not allow the local Red Guards to dictate the course and pace of events. One of the pro-Maoist Chinese newspapers made it quite clear that the Chinese government had no interest in expelling the British; they would therefore check the local radicals. Indeed, the flourishing economic activity in the colony was beneficial to both nations. And another paper argued that while China of course had no intention of relinquishing its sovereignty over greater Hong Kong, any new settlement would have to be achieved with mutual understanding and trust. Again and again they referred to 1997, thirty years from then, as the date when Britain, according to the "unequal treaties" imposed on Imperial China, would be obliged to return the leased territories to their rightful owners.

But in spite of the restoration of order, Leonardo was very worried. He had lost a lot of his self-confidence, and in the evenings he refused to deal with business matters, however urgent, even over the phone. His enthusiasm for his flourishing business concerns waned. One morning he even stayed at home till eleven o'clock, as if he had forgotten that it was a normal working day, and afterwards he fell on his beloved stuffed-bird cupboard like a man possessed and began frantically pushing it from its place. He did this alone, and without even taking the trouble to first remove the denizens of the cupboard from their shelves. They shuddered with every push, and some of them even fell on their beaks. At last the cupboard was ensconced in its new place, with some of the birds standing and others toppled as if shot, their dead eyes full of anxiety at the unexpected change. The boy came to dust the cupboard at the usual time, and when he went up absent-mindedly to the wall where it usually stood and found it gone, he stood rooted to the spot in horror. When he recovered his composure and discovered the cupboard next to the opposite wall he saw it as an ill omen – one more sign among many of the disintegrating status quo.

"*Fan guei lo, fan guei lo* (Foreign devil, foreign devil)," he muttered to himself over and over again like a spell with the power to restore his integrity and confidence as he began dusting the cupboard. And with these words he was expressing what he had thought for years about the white-skinned demons, who were deterred by nothing, however terrible, and to whom nothing was sacred.

The more troubled Leonardo's spirits became, the more Sarina distanced herself from her past. She became more decisive, more alert and some of her old resourcefulness returned. A new notion had come into her mind, and she began taking steps to realize it. "*Eretz Yisrael*, the Land of Israel, is the place," she repeated constantly to herself. And she became more and more convinced that this was the only road for them to take, to leave the colony and go to the Promised Land.

Everyone is called to the Land of Israel at different times and in different words, she thought to herself, and everyone is entitled to realize his right to settle there in his own good time. Ioannina was dead and gone. The Nazi brutes had murdered its Jews; it would never return to what it had once been. The few families that had survived there, wretched and depressed, would never build themselves up there. Her daughters, Bracha and Adina, had married and exchanged magical Greece for cold, remote America. And it was only rarely, very rarely that she received a letter or a telephone call from them. And the Land of Israel, the old dream, suddenly seemed within her grasp. The brief war of 1967, which had ended in a great victory for the Jews, also encouraged her to realize her plan. She became more and more convinced that it was a sign from heaven, it had to be obeyed – and soon. For her the Land of Israel was the land of the Bible, the homeland of the Jewish people, and ever since she was a child she had been encouraged to feel secret and inexplicable longings for it. How she had loved to hear her father speak of this ancient land, on whose holy soil he himself had never been privileged to tread. Although her brother Jochanan's immigration to Palestine over forty years before had come as a severe shock to her, the innocent childhood dream had somewhat faded, but it had never vanished.

As for Leonardo, the Holy Land was for him an abstract, almost fictional entity. If he ever thought about it at all, he visualized it as a blazing desert, in the center of which stood a hill crowned by a building with a magnificent dome, such as he had seen in pictures and postcards, and at the foot of the hill or next to it, the Holy Sepulchre of his Lord. Although he knew that there were also orchards and plantations in the Land of Israel, for their fruits arrived in the markets of almost every country in the world, he didn't really understand how these fruit trees could grow in that blazing heat and without a drop of water. Strange, he thought one evening when Sarina spoke of Israel to him, how little I know about the place.

Ever since the failure of the "revolt" in the colony, Sarina had been mentioning Israel more and more frequently, and Leonardo wondered about her hidden and to him rather strange connection to the Holy Land. Her Jewishness, he had to admit, was as remote and puzzling to him as the Land of Israel and its history.

"My assistant Yuan," he once remarked as they sat relaxing on the veranda of their home, "says that the Jews are money grubbers and that the stinginess of the La-de-ke family with all its money and property is typical of the Jews all over the world."

When Sarina sniggered, trying to hide her anger at his words, and told him that the wealthy "La-de-ke" family, whose name was actually Radak, were well known not only in the Jewish world but also in the colony and the entire region for their philanthropy and good works, Leonardo smiled, raised his hands in a gesture of surrender and said apologetically, "What am I, a theologian?"

Because of the change that had taken place in Sarina (which was noticed not only by Leonardo, but also the Chinese boy), she stopped accompanying her benefactor to church on Sundays, complaining of troublesome aches and pains in her bones and claiming that the cold and the damp in the church made them worse.

On one of these Sundays, when Leonardo was at church and the Chinese boy was spending his day off with his family in the "new territories," the northern parts of the colony, Sarina sat on the armchair in her room and leafed through the prayer book she had inherited from her grandfather. (Recently she had begun delving into the "Greek chest," as Leonardo called the trunk that Bracha and Adina had sent their mother from Ioannina when they had cleared out the house in readiness for their departure for the New World.) Suddenly the phone rang, and when she picked up the receiver, as if conjured up from the deep, she heard the voice of her brother Jochanan who had gone to Palestine so many years ago.

No, it's just a dream; she said to herself and stifled the cry about to burst from her lips: "Jochanan, you're alive! I knew it! I knew it!" She had only seen her brother once after he had left home, when she was an adolescent girl, about a year after the defeat of the Nazis. Jochanan, who was in flight from the British in Palestine, had found a temporary refuge in the Jewish quarter in Ioannina. But by then the town and the Jewish community were no more than a pathetic shadow of what they had once been.

"*Yo kiero vizitarte* (I want to come visit you)," she clearly heard Jochanan's voice saying to her. But no, it wasn't Jochanan, it was a young man who spoke a stilted Ladino with a foreign accent. "*Benhazar kerido?* (Dear Benhazar?)" she said, hesitantly now, sighing, and added in English, "Come here quickly, we want to see you."

She knew, of course, about the existence of this nephew of hers, but she had no idea what he looked like, for he did not appear in any family photograph.

Nor had she ever heard his voice, and she would not have identified it if it hadn't been so similar to that of her brother, who was in the habit of phoning once a year, before the High Holidays. Tears of happiness flooded her eyes.

All day Sarina waited tensely for Benhazar to arrive. And to help her relax she poured herself a drink, which was unusual for her.

"Benhazar Cohen," she murmured to herself, "*ijo de mi ermano Jochanan, sovrino mio, ojos mios tu, ven, ven presto* (My brother Jochanan's son, my nephew, my eyes, come quickly)."

A light squealing of brakes and a slamming door made her spring to her feet. Even as she hurried to the open window she heard hurried footsteps on the staircase.

Tall and dark-skinned Benhazar stood before her. Sarina fell on his neck and kissed him, close to tears. It was Jochanan himself standing before her, she thought. And for a moment she went back forty years in time, and said voicelessly, "Jochanan has come home, he's sorry for leaving mother and father and me. Jochanan can't live without us." She was back in Ioannina of the old, prewar days, with the long black plait of which she had been so proud then. Even the spotted dress she had worn on the day they parted from Jochanan came back to clothe her body. Jochanan was back, and this time she wouldn't let him go. And in her heart time stopped, the Holocaust never happened, and her life took a different course, without the mistakes of the past. And after a moment, when the illusion faded, she made up her mind to adopt Benhazar as her son and to do everything in her power to help him. My daughters have left me and in their place Benhazar has been sent to me, flesh of my flesh, to be my son.

And aloud she said, "*Avla i rekonte-me komo se sientan todos en Yerushalayim* (Speak and tell me how everybody in Jerusalem is doing)."

Chapter Three

After my unproductive meeting with Major Holmes I spent glum days in Oxford. The walls of the colleges seemed closed against me. None of the veterans of the war in the East, whose names I gathered one by one, were willing to meet me and tell me about my father. News of Jochanan's son who had come to open old wounds had apparently spread. As in the days of my childhood, during the War of Independence and after it, I felt the energy draining out of me and a black mood, which Aunt Flora used to call *strechura*, settled on my heart. Even then I knew that once *strechura* descended on you it was in no hurry to depart. I was overcome by a great weakness and I remembered a traumatic experience one distant summer in the seaside town of Netanya.

My father and I were staying in a small hotel, and one hot morning we were walking down the main street on our way to the beach. I was wearing a tight old bathing suit made of wool, I felt hot and sweaty, and I was eager to jump into the waves and show my father what an excellent swimmer I was, after the swimming lessons I had recently completed at the Jerusalem YMCA. And as if to spite me and spoil my fun, one of my father's mysterious friends suddenly crossed our path. A stern-looking man with a broad-brimmed hat tilted over his brow. He greeted us briefly, without showing any pleasure or surprise, and immediately began shooting out short sentences like machine-gun bursts. My father listened to him patiently for a few minutes which seemed to me like an eternity, and then answered him quietly, speaking so slowly that it almost drove me mad. My father ignored my demonstrations of impatience, for this time too, as always, there was something more urgent and important on his agenda than me.

But I had other plans. Little by little, kicking a small stone I found on the pavement, I inched away from them and hid behind a bush, and when I saw that they weren't looking, I ran down to the beach. I shook off my sandals, threw my shirt onto the sand, and charged into the waiting waves. With my whole body immersed in the water I was in the seventh heaven of delight. I swam out further and further from the shore.

After a while, feeling extremely pleased with myself, I raised my head and with slightly stinging eyes I looked around. There was nothing to be seen but quiet waves surrounding me on all sides. I strained my eyes and looked again in all directions, and after a while I managed to make out the lifeguard's tower, tiny and blurred and very far away. Panic gripped me. A cold sweat broke out on my forehead. With all my might I began swimming to the shore. The light wind that was blowing didn't help me now – however energetically I beat the water with my arms and legs the waves returned me to where I was before, and I made no progress whatsoever. All I wanted now was to be back with my father, even if I had to listen to his boring, incomprehensible conversation with his friend. But instead I was increasingly swept to the side. A big wave bathed my face and bitter, salty water filled my mouth and throat. I felt the strength draining out of me. My head sank and all my efforts to keep it above the water failed – heavy weights were pulling my legs down to the depths. The water surrounded me like a wall and threatened to suck me into the whirlpools created by the currents.

Suddenly a mighty hand seized hold of me and dragged my limp, defeated body to the shore, where my father was waiting for me in his pale grey suit, with the gentle little waves, which only a few moments before had threatened to swallow me, lapping the toes of his black shoes. He stood there alone, and before I fainted at his feet I heard him whisper something, uncharacteristically, in Ladino.

And now too, in Hong Kong, my aunt spoke to me in Ladino, repeating her question: "*Komo se sientan todos en Yerushalayim?* (How's everyone in Jerusalem?)"

I stood before her unable to utter a word. I was still stunned by my sudden decision to fly to the Far East, by the flight itself, by the meeting which seemed to be taking place in a dream, and also by Sarina's features which bore such a striking resemblance to those of my father. She was a female version, charming and smiling, of the man I had lost and was seeking with might and main. Never had I felt the mysterious power of history manifest itself in flesh and blood as I did before this impressive woman. One more quick glance and I had already internalized the beauty of her slightly wrinkled face, her abundant black hair streaked with grey. And suddenly I understood things that I had always tried to understand and never succeeded until today. With my eyes I caressed her hair, her tilted nose, her noble chin, her perfect figure. Afterwards I looked around and was surprised by the luxury of the house, its furniture and its vaguely mysterious atmosphere. Taking two or three steps in the spacious living room I caught a glimpse of a heavy black cupboard, polished to a shine, whose gleaming glass doors displayed exotic stuffed birds.

A sense of strangeness took hold of me, even though there was nothing cold or depressing about the room but on the contrary, the atmosphere was warm and even cozy. Sarina was so like my father that for a moment it seemed to me that my father was about to emerge from some hiding place in the large living room, or from one of the other rooms, open his arms, as he used to do in my childhood, and call, "Who's coming to Daddy?" and then raise me high in the air, rub his head against my belly, and laugh aloud...

I felt giddy.

Sarina apparently sensed my agitation, the confusion and emotion which were paralyzing me, and with a slight movement of her hand she invited me to sit down on an armchair upholstered in bright silk. I sank into it, exhausted but full of hope that after all my disappointments I was finally about to learn the truth.

Even though she didn't ask, I felt obliged to give Sarina a reason for my presence in Hong Kong, and I muttered something about a conference at the university. I could hardly have told her that in the madness that had taken hold of me I had spent almost all my savings on journeys into my father's past.

Then I told her a little about the family in Jerusalem. I did not mention either my dead father or my distant mother. The entry into the room of the Chinese boy, who had cut short his holiday, as if he sensed that there was an urgent need of his services, interrupted me. He was holding a tray with cold drinks, dainty sandwiches, and a selection of exotic fruits. He was evidently infected by his mistress's excitement – he almost tripped twice while serving the refreshments. I attempted to engrave his appearance on my memory, but before I could do so a silly question occurred to me and distracted my attention: did Sarina still keep a kosher kitchen?

As she sat opposite me she reminded me of the Sephardi ladies of Rechavia, my father's relatives, with their black hair and smooth faces, beautiful as Madonnas in spite of the cruel lines etched on them by age. Although I knew that these Sephardi aunts came from the courtyards of the Old City, Mekor

Baruch, and the older quarters of Jerusalem, strolling past the sundial in Jaffa Street, between the Machane Yehuda police station and the market in their girlhood – a far cry from the aristocratic, tree-shaded suburb of Rechavia – I nevertheless insisted on calling them, perhaps because I was so young then, "the Sephardi ladies of Rechavia."

When I finally began to tell her about my father's death, the Chinese servant glided out of the room (I could swear that he literally glided an inch above the floor). First I described the terrible fire that broke out in the study where he secluded himself to write his scholarly papers. Afterwards, with minute and inexplicable attention to detail, I described the actions of the firemen and their savage behavior. I dwelt on this even more than on the deterioration in my father's health which had taken place shortly before the fire. Still avoiding any mention of my mother, I turned quickly to the second generation of the family. I told her about my cousin on my mother's side, Ruby, in other words Dr. Robert Levy, who had studied medicine abroad and was now engaged in important research at the university hospital; about Danino, who held an important government job; about Armelito, who had tried his hand at complicated business deals and failed.

And so I went on, dredging up long-forgotten childhood experiences, reviewing the exploits and achievements of close and distant kinsfolk, and at the same time saying to myself: how strange, do I really have to tell all this to Aunt Sarina? She herself is a part of Rechavia, no less a foundation stone of the neighborhood than Eliezer Yellin, the founder of the neighborhood, himself. Even the fact that Sarina knew no Hebrew now seemed astonishing to me, for I had seen her likeness dozens of times making her way with her baskets from Rosh-Rechavia on Keren Kayemet Street to Reznik's pharmacy on Azza Street.

Sarina smiled apologetically, as if she could read my thoughts. In Balkan English, peppered with words in Greek, and in a Ladino unlike that spoken in Jerusalem, she went on questioning me. My excitement at the meeting grew from minute to minute.

Even though she was still relatively young, she reminded me of Clara, a relation I used to visit with my father as a child, in the neighborhood of Mekor Baruch. The cadence of her speech, the expression on her face and her behavior in general were unsuited to her time: she seemed to have emerged from an old photograph in a family album and put on flesh in order to play tricks on me.

Suddenly, as if sensing that I was betraying my mission and not doing what I was supposed to do, I said, "*Konte-me la istoria de mi padre* (Tell me my father's story)." And in English I added, "I want to know more. I must know more."

Sarina smiled as if she had been waiting for this turn of events. "I know that you didn't come here for a scientific conference. It was me you were seeking and to me that you came. And it makes me proud and happy."

Her personality won my heart. For the first time in my life I was seized with longing for the person sitting opposite me. Or perhaps this too was only another illusion of the magical world into which I had stepped? I felt a strange urge to turn my head and look behind my shoulder – perhaps some magic door had really opened and my father had stolen into the room?

I sat in silence and after a rather long pause Sarina began to tell me about her parents' home and her childhood in Ioannina, until the bitter day when her brother left them and emigrated to the Land of Israel. Only now I understood how hard it had been for her to part from her beloved brother Jochanan, and how deeply his abandonment had wounded her. With great sensitivity she described the effects of his departure not only on her adolescent heart, but also on the vague dream of the Land of Israel which had been instilled in her since childhood. After that she spoke about the Jewish quarter near the lake on whose banks the town of Ioannina was built.

"The Jewish community was traditional and observant," she said and a faint, enigmatic smile appeared on her lips. "We lived in narrow alleys, near the castle of Ali Pasha."

About her father, my grandfather Albert, she said that he was a traveling salesman who made the rounds of the towns of northern Greece. At first he traveled from village to village in a cart drawn by two horses, and later on, when his business prospered, he exchanged the cart for a motor car. He was one of the first people in his little town to acquire a car. In her story she mentioned towns like Larissa and Igoumenitsa, and even little country towns like Arta and Preveza where there were small Jewish communities, but mainly she spoke of Salonika, where her father went once a week at least. He would sell sesame seeds, raw hides, silkworms and wool, and buy all kinds of fabrics for his customers, and later even iron and machines. Enthusiastically she described her first visit to Salonika, the gateway to the great world, stressing and stressing again the vast difference between this big city and the provincial Ioannina with its single synagogue.

When she spoke of the synagogue and the courtyard with the Sukkoth booth in its center, she explained with a smile that every year before the festival of Sukkoth there was an argument between the dignitaries and sages of the congregation with regard to the compliance of this booth with the ritual requirements. Although the walls and roof were permanently covered with trailing green vines, some people argued that this was not sufficient and that it should be covered with an additional layer of fresh branches, and her father, who was not a stickler for tradition but did not dismiss it lightly either, would lay a few palm fronds on top of the vines and thus make the booth kosher in the eyes of the entire congregation.

She described her father as if he were standing in front of her, alive and kicking in his best blue-striped suit. On Saturdays and Holy Days he would wear an antique gold watch on an impressive chain on the waistcoat encasing his large paunch. He walked the neighborhood alleys like a king, she said, and she began to tell me about the roots of the family and its pedigree, about its connection to Lazar Balali, who was an important expert on the Hebrew language, and a professor of Jewish studies in the arts faculty of the University of Salonika, and to Rabbi Davos of Ioannina, who had died during the German occupation, about their friendship with the merchant Shabtai Cabili, in whose home they often spent the festivals and holidays, and who had also perished in the Holocaust, and about the genial Yosef Eliyahu who was a well-known poet in the Greek language, esteemed by both Jews and Greeks. And the names kept on coming as the floodgates of her memory opened, and she spoke too of the Carasso, Tiano, Vinizia, Haviv, Modiano, Molcho, Matalon families and more and more.

As she spoke she gazed straight ahead of her, but when during the course of this magical journey into the depths of the past her eyes encountered mine, she was for some reason assailed by doubts that she had lost my attention, and immediately, with an apologetic smile, she adopted a more businesslike tone and began to give me a detailed description of the day when Jochanan had left Ioannina.

"I am ten years younger than Jochanan," she said, "and as I have already told you, the shock of his departure went on haunting me for a long time – until a far worse catastrophe, the Nazi invasion, some fifteen years later, dulled the pain of our abandonment by my brother Jochanan." Tears choked her throat and she did not suppress her tears and said, "I only saw Jochanan one more time, Benazariko, only one more time."

I trembled, profoundly affected by the warm, motherly pet name, "Benazariko," which my aunt on my father's side, in Jerusalem, used to call me in my childhood. But my emotion did not diminish my eagerness to hear why my father had returned that one time to Ioannina.

"They shot at the British. He and his friend apparently did something terrible. But if Jochanan felt obliged to do what he did, I have no doubt that there was no alternative, that they had to do it. And after they did it they had to disappear fast. His friend stayed there, in Palestine, and Jochanan came home, to us.

"It was in the summer of 1946. Ioannina was then a ghost town. We, the Jews who had remained alive, walked around like corpses activated by some mysterious invisible force. When we recovered from the shock of the meeting, Jochanan asked about relatives, friends and acquaintances, and the answer was always the same: tortured, murdered, shot, deported, exterminated. Now I can admit that some invisible barrier separated me from Jochanan from the minute he set foot in the town.

"Coming from *Eretz Yisrael*, he did not understand my words, was unable to grasp the dimensions of the catastrophe that had descended on us. Even though he knew what had happened, he didn't understand the full horror of it. The image of the old Ioannina was engraved on his heart, and he refused to part from it. He returned to the hidden corners where we had played as children, and repeated stories of his childhood exploits. He saw the town, the neighborhood, the community, and even me, his sister, as a kind of nature reserve, a museum piece, a monument to his past. We were the past and he – the present and the future. He was incapable of accepting the fact that twenty years had passed since he abandoned our father, our mother and me, and in the meantime the terrible Holocaust had taken place. Even when he tried, he didn't know how to ask the right questions, he latched onto insignificant details and avoided the main issue, as if deliberately. Even though he knew that our father had been murdered and our mother had been snatched from us and sent to Birkenau, it seemed to me that for some reason, in the depths of his heart, he was angry with me, with Mother, with Father, and in fact the entire population of northern Greece at the time. It seemed to me like a kind of arrogance, which I couldn't explain then, or now. His whole family had been in hell and he had been far away, in *Eretz Yisrael*, absorbed in his own affairs."

Here Sarina paused, and then, choosing her words with care, she said, "At an improvised road block the Nazi beasts murdered your grandfather. He was on his way home from Igoumenitsa. Someone from the Moisis family, who was hiding nearby, saw the bloodthirsty savages cut him down. We sent the news to Palestine, but to this day I don't know where Jochanan was at the time.

"When he returned to Ioannina it was as if he blamed us. Not with words but with the look in his eyes. How could he accuse us of passivity, of apathy, of cowardice, when there were heroes among us who opposed the brutes and even paid with their lives? And when he himself did not come to Ioannina as a hero but far from it – he came to hide in the town of his childhood, to ask us for sanctuary and protection. When strangers came to Ioannina he would go underground and stay in hiding for days on end without daring to leave the house. In the daytime he played with little Bracha and Adina, and at night he would listen to our stories about the Jewish partisans who joined the Greeks in the mountains and fought like lions. About himself he said little, and we learned nothing about his life or his role in the Jewish struggle in Palestine. *Para ti es solo istoria, para mozotros es la istoria de muestra vida* (For you this is only history, for us it's the story of our lives)," Sarina concluded sadly.

Evening fell and the Chinese boy appeared with his featherduster to dust the cupboard containing the stuffed birds, as if it were a shrine to the spirits of the family ancestors. He performed his task punctiliously and reverently, and it was evident that his master's homecoming was an event that gave rise to a certain excitement in him. From the kitchen a faint aroma of frying wafted into the room, and I knew that dinnertime was near. The preparations for Leonardo's arrival intensified, and at last he arrived.

Leonardo Reil cut an aloof and imposing figure, and for some reason he reminded me of the honorary consul of Austria in Jerusalem. Was it his combed-back grey hair, the striped suit on his lean body, the pale-pink handkerchief sticking out of his jacket pocket, or perhaps the pointed black shoes? For a moment I sat still, looking up at the "consul," and then I rose from my seat and approached him with my hand outstretched. Sarina too stood up and in an excitement which to myself I dubbed "Mediterranean" she cried: "Leonardo, this is Benhazar, my brother Jochanan's son. He suddenly arrived from Israel, without letting us know in advance. What a surprise! Look at him, Leonardo, look at him, that's exactly what Jochanan looked like when he left us forty years ago."

"Pleased to meet you," I said and held out my hand. "In Israel people call me Benhazar. In Hebrew it means 'son of the stranger.' It's a nickname my friends gave me after they saw my father for the first time."

Leonardo shook my hand warmly and said, "I'm glad to meet you, Benhazar. I hope they've given you something to drink."

"Thank you," I replied, "I've already tasted the strange fruits you have here too."

Leonardo smiled and sat down in his armchair and immediately began a polite conversation, asking me about my occupation, my army service and the situation in the Middle East.

Sarina left the room and our conversation soon petered out. We sat facing each other in silence, two distant strangers.

Chapter Four

Sarina was overwhelmed by memories of the terrible days of the war. The arrival of her nephew, the news of whose birth in Palestine had reached them when the Germans entered Ioannina, in September 1943, revived forgotten scenes which she thought would never return to haunt her. Now she relived the Italian attack on Greece, in the winter of 1940, and the terrible fears for those closest to her, especially little Bracha and Adina; again she heard the rabbi's sermon in the synagogue and the ghastly hints it contained; and again she was thrilled by the courage of the Jewish youths who had joined the war effort and stood up against the invader. The figure of Yaakov Uziel, who had fallen in battle, rose vividly before her eyes. She remembered how she had tried to catch his eye in the synagogue when she was a child, and the "Promenade," the broad street where the adolescent boys and girls strolled on Saturday nights, stealing shy looks at one another. Once, when she was already a young girl, promenading with her parents, her eyes had met his again. How kind and gentle his look had been then, but she had been overcome with embarrassment and had turned her eyes away.

In the early days of the war her husband Shlomo had begun to go downhill. He was not yet forty, but in her young eyes he seemed like an old man, with the settled views and authority of his years, and his decline therefore seemed to her natural. So she remembered her father too, and also, dimly, her grandfather. Shlomo took less and less interest in his family, and after that he lost interest in his shop as well. He sat withdrawn into himself behind the counter or in the house, and all her attempts to encourage him were in vain. Little by little she took over the business and the burden of earning a living.

Bitterly she now remembered her joy at the first news of the success of the Greek army in pushing the Italians back to the middle of Albania, and her pride in being Greek: she had spoken Greek in preference to Ladino, read Greek literature and taken pride in the heritage of classical Greece, which had been so alien to her as a child at school. But the joy of victory had been short-lived; soon reports began coming in of casualties, including the names of young men from the Jewish families she knew so well. After a few weeks the Jewish wounded and maimed began returning to Ioannina. Eliyahu Bracha, her neighbor, came home with chest and leg wounds, and at night she would hear his screams, screams she would never forget. The hard times had begun.

Connections with Jochanan were completely cut off. It was as if she saw him through a dense veil, and when she tried to picture his face his features escaped her, one by one: when she saw his brow and curls, his eyes disappeared, and when they came back to her, she lost sight of his mouth and chin.

On the eighth of April 1941 her father Albert went on a routine business trip to Salonika. Two days later he returned, stunned and broken. Peeping through the shutters of his friend Daniel's house, he had seen the German tanks entering the town. The Greek forces had abandoned Salonika shortly before this in order to regroup and mount a defensive operation (or so they claimed). The representatives of the government in Athens had also left. A few days later grim news began to trickle in from Salonika. The Jewish newspapers had stopped coming out, the Ladino *Messajero* no longer reached the neighborhood, and on every corner the Greek *Apoievamatini* spewed its pro-Nazi, anti-Semitic poison. Her father stopped going on business trips, sat at home, and paid occasional visits to Shlomo at their house or in the shop. The two of them were experts at picking up news about the German advances and exploits, as if they were endowed with sensitive antennae. And the worse the news, the more satisfaction – an almost apocalyptic satisfaction – they seemed to derive from it, much to the surprise and concern of Sarina, who found their obsession with the news unbalanced and morbid.

One afternoon they told her about the arrest of the leaders of the Jewish community in Salonika: Charles Bracha, Albert Arditi, Shlomo Uziel, and Shaltiel Cohen. The names of Jewish prisoners now came in a constant stream: Raphael Menashe, Yitzchak Shaki, Shaul Molcho, Albert Jinio. Bad news came over the telephone too, and worst of all were the stories told by the refugees who had succeeded in escaping from the German zone and reaching the area occupied by the Italians. The Italian zone included Ioannina. Moving from one zone to the other involved great danger, and the Jews who arrived safely in Ioannina went to the synagogue to give thanks for their deliverance.

Sarina remembered how the news reached them of the arrest of two Jewish employees in the American consulate in Salonika: David Tiano and Emanuel Carasso (David was shot in February 1942 and Emanuel was severely tortured). And before long they heard too of the "Rosenberg Unit" (a name which did not mean much to her at the time) and the racial laws. And then came the news of the concentration of the Jews in the great Freedom Square in Salonika one Saturday morning and the selection of those able to work for the Reich. All day long they stood there in the heat, without food or drink, and anyone who collapsed or fainted was punished by vicious kicks. If the kicks didn't bring them around the Germans poured cold water on them, and forced them to caper like clowns and perform humiliating exercises, crawl on their bellies and dance to the whistle of a young Nazi storm trooper. German and even a few Greek girls laughed and clapped. The Greek refugee who told this story only a few days after the event wept bitterly, but his audience, even though their hearts contracted with rage and fear, did not yet grasp the dimensions of the horror.

The infamous names of Wisliceny, Brunner, Gerbin, and Doctor Merten reached Ioannina together with the news of the decree regarding the yellow star, the prohibition against riding in trams, using the telephone and other similar restrictions.

Contact with Salonika was cut off almost entirely, but nevertheless the fearful news filtered through, and the Jews of Ioannina lived the events in the big city and sensed the evil coming closer, but they had no way of escaping. The hatred for Rabbi Dr. Koretz, appointed by the occupiers to head the Jewish community of Salonika, grew. He urged his flock to obey the orders of their persecutors and the youths of Ioannina were up in arms: how dared he?

But their elders rebuked them for speaking ill of a rabbi, and there were even a few pious Jews who argued fervently that the punishment that had descended on the sinful city was well deserved, and that it was God's will that this den of vice, this Sodom and Gomorrah, should reap the fruits of its sins, but there was no way that the holy congregation of Ioannina, and other small and God-fearing congregations in the north of Greece, would suffer a similar fate. These false prophets came up with all kinds of peculiar arguments to prove their case, and even claimed that for reasons of practical politics alone there was no danger to Ioannina: "For who would take the trouble to persecute a handful of Jews scattered around the Greek countryside? Haven't the Germans got anything more important and urgent to do at this moment in time, when a mighty war is being waged all over Europe? Salonika cannot be seen as a precedent – whatever they did to the Jews there was only to serve as a warning to the Jews and Greeks in other parts of the country, and from now on everything will return to normal. And besides, we're under Italian rule here, and what have these Latins, who we know so well, to do with the Aryan racial laws?"

After the ghettos were set up in Salonika and the Jews were imprisoned in them, they began to hear of transportations to an unknown destination; the complacent elders of Ioannina argued that even if the information was true, all it involved was banishment to Cracow in Poland, and when this accursed war was over everyone would come home again. After all, said Sarina to herself as the memories returned, none of us had seen the sealed cattle cars with our own eyes, none of us had felt the jackboots of the Nazi brutes and the blows of the Gestapo on our own flesh – why shouldn't we have believed the self-appointed "authorities" of Ioannina? And she conjured up the images of the most prominent of these "authorities," as she called them to herself, who in a short time, a very short time, would themselves become the victims. What they thought and said then, she did not know, of course.

She stayed where she was.

Gradually the race laws were applied to Jewish communities outside Salonika in the German zone. The Bulgarians too joined in the murder and mayhem with their German benefactors. And the Jews of Ioannina thanked their lucky stars that they were in the Italian zone. And indeed, when the Italian soldiers reached Ioannina, they turned out to be much more moderate than all the others, just as her husband Shlomo and her father Albert had predicted, and little by little their fears died down. These Latins were easygoing and apathetic, and although they paid occasional lip service to the race laws (one proclamation, plastered on the wall of the house on the corner of their street, rose for a moment before Sarina's eyes), they did little to enforce them and left the Jews alone.

But in September 1943, after the Italian surrender, the situation changed radically. The Germans took over the Italian zone. At the beginning there were still Jews in Ioannina who continued to believe that no harm would come to them, for they were Greeks in every respect and not at all like their brothers in Salonika: quiet, modest, submissive, even patriotic. And they were on good terms with their Greek neighbors too. All these things increased their sense of security and the illusion that after the defeat in Africa the Germans would have neither the time nor the will to persecute the Jews and destroy them.

"We committed suicide," thought Sarina. When she thought of Benhazar ("My child, a brand saved from the burning, a son of the destroyed Ioannina") the tears choked her throat.

Suddenly she saw Jochanan's desertion of Ioannina in a new light. For the first time she understood the categorical imperative that had made her brother leave the town of his birth and abandon his family and herself, his sister Sarina. It was no caprice, no hardheartedness or denial of his nearest and dearest which had taken him away from them to the Land of Israel. Now she thought of the great war that had broken out there the previous year – the "Six-Day War" as the Israelis called it. The echoes of that war had reached her, and here in this remote colony she too had been swept up in the enthusiasm that had seized hold of world Jewry with the liberation of the Western Wall and Rachel's Tomb. In her imagination she saw these two sites side by side and Jews with beards (like the elders of the Ioannina synagogue) praying there, while women (like her neighbors in the Jewish quarter and their mothers) came to pour out their hearts to the matriarch Rachel.

CHAPTER FOUR

For a moment she saw the Land of Israel as *Agrapa*, one of those remote, inaccessible sanctuaries in the mountains of Greece where the inhabitants escaped registration and paying taxes. These mountain sanctuaries were relatively safe even during the war, and Rabbi Barzilai, the chief rabbi of Athens, had escaped there. And Jochanan too had escaped to a sacred, imaginary *Agrapa* in the East in his youth.

"And you, Benhazar," she said voicelessly, "are the fruit of that escape, the fruit of the sanctuary in *Eretz Yisrael*."

Jochanan was a stranger in Ioannina, and apparently he was a stranger in the Land of Israel too, for otherwise why should the British, the Arabs and the Jews have united to persecute him? Why had he lived in constant fear? Looking behind his shoulder to see if anyone was coming to stick a knife in his back? Why had he been consumed by fire in his room? "*Sagapo, agrapa mia* (I love you, my sanctuary)," Sarina played with the words.

In thirty cattle cars the Jews of Athens were transported, packed like sardines, and on the way the train of death collected more Jews from Larissa, Volos, Trikala and Ioannina. Thus their numbers grew until they reached nearly three thousand. One hundred to a rail car. "*Adio, Senyor del Mundo* (Oh God, Master of the world), and where was I, my daughters and my husband?"

The train continued on its way, joined by more and more Jews, from Macedonia, Yugoslavia and Hungary, after which it passed through Austria and reached the German border. In the middle of the journey about two hundred people were taken off and led on foot to Bergen-Belsen, and the rest were taken to Auschwitz – where an ancient love song that had wandered with the Jews from Spain received a new, ghastly meaning. They sang and wept: "*Torno i digo, ke va ser de mi?* (Again I repeat, what will become of me?)"

Sarina returned in her thoughts to that terrible day in October 1943. Early in the morning the municipal workers of Ioannina hung up notices ordering the Jews to present themselves for registration. Until that day the Germans had not enforced the race laws in the town. The tension grew from hour to hour. Even the incurable optimists were silenced now, and all over northern Greece people began scurrying from place to place like mice in a trap. Some of those who left the town came back a few days later, scared to death.

On that fateful day, close to noon, Hans came into the shop, wearing the uniform of a German officer, the insignia of rank on his shoulders and the visor of his elegant cap adorned with a braided gold ribbon. As she learned later, he was a senior officer in the command of the regiment stationed in the town. His eyes were blue, his gaze level but gentle, his nose slightly snub and his mouth pleasant. Shlomo wasn't in the shop; he had gone to talk to her father who was sitting in the neighborhood café, and Sarina stood behind the counter sipping strong black coffee. She had been hard at work all morning, clearing shelves for the new cotton shirts that had by some miracle arrived the evening before from Salonika, and soon she would have to go home to take care of Bracha and Adina.

When Hans entered the shop they looked at each other for a moment, and then he bowed politely and asked in German (or was it in English?), "This shop belongs to the Cohen family, if I am not mistaken?"

"Yes," she replied in Greek, and afterwards in Spanish and English.

A shiver she would never forget ran down her spine. And he went on to ask her the first names of the members of the family, this time in fluent English.

"Shlomo, Sarina, Bracha, Adina," she said in growing dread.

CHAPTER FOUR

He took out a notebook and wrote, repeating the names aloud and spelling them.

"Is Daniel Cohen also a family relation?"

"No," she said, shaking her head emphatically. And she immediately thought: Who knows if I won't be sorry for giving their names? And on second thought: And perhaps on the contrary, I would regret having hidden them.

With an indifferent expression Hans glanced around the shelves, and without another word he turned on his heel and left the shop. It seemed to her that she saw a faint smile on his lips.

Sarina remained standing behind the counter, trembling all over.

Don't just stand there, she commanded herself, don't sit down! Walk, move, and don't stop moving! And like a caged lioness she began running to and fro in the shop. And suddenly, as if someone had opened the door of the cage, she burst outside into the street. She looked around, trying to find the German officer who had disappeared, and then ran to the café which, for the first time in her life, she entered. She rushed to the table where Shlomo and Albert were sitting with Yaakov Cassuto from Larissa and someone from the Yakuel family whose name she did not remember. The eyes of everyone present turned to her as if in answer to some silent command. A woman in the café, in the morning?! What next?! asked the scandalized expressions on the faces of the habitués, the merchants and the loafers, who came there every morning. "A German officer came to the shop," she blurted out to Shlomo, with terror in her eyes. "He wanted to know the names of the girls, asked about someone called Daniel Cohen, and wrote everything down in his notebook. *Me voy murir, Solomon, me voy murir* (I'm going to die, Shlomo, I'm going to die)."

Sarina's words were greeted with astonishment. Everyone was already upset by the order to register the members of the Jewish community at the municipal offices. Their hearts were full of anger and fear. Many had urged the leaders of the congregation to go to the army headquarters and complain, to try to make them change their minds. And here was more trouble. A German officer dared to address a Jewish woman when she was alone in her shop and question her about her family!

"*Ken es Daniel Cohen?* (Who is Daniel Cohen?)" asked Yaakov Cassuto.

Nobody recognized the name. The only Daniel Cohen they knew was the five-year-old son of the barber Nechemia at the end of the street. Suddenly Sarina, Shlomo and Albert remembered the deserted shop with the door wide open, and they rose and hurried out of the café. They reached the shop at a run and stood there for a long time scanning the shelves and walls as if trying to find a clue to the officer's intentions.

"Lock up at once," ordered Albert. They went home and waited in suspense, like the rest of the congregation, for the German response to the deputation of their representatives.

Later that afternoon they heard to their amazement that the deputation had been graciously received. Two officers whose rank was unknown to the Jewish representatives immediately agreed that they had been unjustly treated. And the commander of the regiment, who joined them a little later, summoned the mayor, rebuked him for the heartless proclamation, and promised solemnly that the race laws would not be applied to the Jews of Ioannina.

The Jews breathed a sigh of relief, and Chananya the "songster" took up his place in the synagogue courtyard, a stick in his hand and a new song on his lips:

CHAPTER FOUR

> *And Mordechai went out*
> *from the presence of the king*
> *In royal apparel of blue and white*
> *and a great crown of gold,*
> *And with a garment of fine linen and purple;*
> *And the city of Shushan rejoiced and was glad.*
> *The Jews had light and gladness and joy and honor.*

Even little Bracha and Adina, who up to now had clung to their mother and refused to leave her side, as if they sensed the gravity of the situation, were reassured and went out with all the other children, laughing merrily, to parade through the neighborhood with Chananya.

The complacency reached new heights. "No harm will come to our community," Sarina heard the synagogue treasurer say to his friend one morning as she stood on her veranda and shook out a carpet.

"Shame on the young men for running away," said Elisha the tanner, as he passed by, and in a voice full of hostility he added, "Running off to join the underground, the Communists! They're robbing us of our young, the anti-Semites! *Por ke, dios mio, ay ke fuir de los alemanes?* (What reason, my God, is there to run away from the Germans?)"

And Sarina continued with her daily routine, but her heart was full of dread. She saw Hans from time to time, driving past in an army car, combing the streets of the town. This car, she noted, was not full of stiff, helmeted soldiers with stony expressions on their faces, like the other cars carrying troops; it had something attractive, almost sporty about it, in spite of the pale-faced Hans sitting there stiffly in his pressed uniform. Sometimes he sat in the seat next to the driver, a young soldier sitting straight backed and stern faced as he held the wheel.

And once she saw him on foot walking down the commercial street, studying the shop signs and writing energetically in the notebook she remembered so well. The young driver walked a few paces behind him, like a servant, or a bodyguard. It appeared that Hans had to report on what was happening in the commercial center, or perhaps only on the activities of the Jews. She never learned exactly what his function was. But one thing she sensed very clearly: whenever he passed by her shop he slowed his steps, looked carefully around him, and stole a quick glance inside. Was it her he was looking for behind the counter?

On Thursday the twenty-third of March 1944 it happened. Sarina was busy preparing for the Sabbath. She never left the house on a Thursday. Like her mother and grandmother before her she devoted the day to cooking, baking and making the house ready to receive the holy Sabbath. Thursday, *jueves,* was longer than all the other days of the week, and even when the lights went on in the town and Shlomo and the girls had gone to bed, she still had work to do. She polished the pots and pans, washed the floors, and cleaned the Sabbath hot plate. Weariness and a profound melancholy were etched on her face, but also a sense of satisfaction in doing her duty and continuing an age-old tradition. In the end she went through all the rooms, scrutinizing every nook and cranny: here she had to add a little oil to the lamp, there the tablecloth was creased and she had to smooth it with her hand or press it with the iron heating on the stove, and then she looked in on her sleeping daughters again and straightened a blanket or a pillow.

Suddenly she heard a knock on the kitchen window. At first the knocks were soft and hesitant, but gradually they grew more insistent and aggressive. In the dim light coming from the little window she saw the outline of a man standing in her garden. She trembled, her heart pounded, but she stood rooted to the spot, mesmerized. There was no doubt about it, she said to herself, it was the German officer. How strange Hans looked without the peaked cap on his head! How pathetic! At first she wanted to call her husband and denounce the German's impudence at the top of her voice, but she immediately had second thoughts and almost without fear she went up to the window to see what he wanted. He beckoned her to come closer with one hand, while laying the index finger of the other on his lips as a sign for her to keep quiet. Some inner instinct told her to obey him. She took another step, and another towards the kitchen window, holding a wet towel in her hand.

The tension in the officer's face relaxed.

"Open the window," he said.

She did as he bade her and a kind of shy smile appeared on his lips. Now too she noticed for the first time how his eyes were shining. His face was bathed in perspiration but it was still very handsome. He had a snub nose and blue eyes. A man of her own age. Young and decisive.

"Come to the shop tonight. Please."

She recoiled, and her face revealed her fear and revulsion.

"You don't understand," he went on in his heavy accent, "this is your only chance to save yourself and your family, your little girls, Bracha and Adina. Yes, you must bring them too and also your husband Shlomo, and hide there, because tomorrow they are going to expel all the Jews. This is the last minute, the very last."

Sarina thought immediately of her father, who had set out the day before for Igoumenitsa and was due back the next day.

"And my father? and my mother?" she asked aloud.

Hans silenced her gently – apparently he did not understand her question – and raising his eyes to her face, since his head, from where he stood, was level with her chest, he said chivalrously, "My name is Hans. I'll come to see you in the shop. I'll look after you. And you, lock yourselves up and don't come out. Remember, don't go outside on any account."

And he disappeared into the darkness of the garden.

Sarina remained standing at the open window.

"Mister Officer," she whispered, when she had recovered slightly from the shock, "Hans, please come back."

Outside there was only silence and darkness.

For seven months Sarina and Shlomo and their two little girls hid in the family shop, locked from the inside, seven months which lasted an eternity and were full of horror. It was their private concentration camp. Apart from Hans nobody knew they were there. Once every two days he would drop food and water into the back window of the shop: strolling innocently through the shops and warehouses of the deserted commercial center he would casually drop the parcel, which looked like a bag of rubbish, into the window. Sarina would collect it and in the darkness of the shop she would share the meager rations out between her family, taking only the leftovers for herself. It seemed that only her concern for her family and the heavy burden of responsibility she had taken on herself sustained her body and kept her going.

During the last weeks of their incarceration, when the cold and stifling oppression deepened, they hardly exchanged a word. Each of them huddled in his corner, his head buried in his hands, waiting for the nightmare to end.

A number of times Shlomo lost control and threatened to give himself up to the authorities. He would rather die than remain imprisoned in this cold, dark dungeon, surrounded by worn-out merchandise, he said wildly. And Sarina would calm him down and watch him with an eagle eye, lest he bring disaster down on the heads of their daughters. For herself and her future she hardly spared a thought. She had one purpose and one purpose only: to save her family. She took no interest in her own welfare, her own desires, and this selflessness was the source of her strength, and made the daily struggle easier to bear. Even during the long nights she would wake up every couple of hours to caress her daughters with her eyes and listen to their even breathing as they slept, and to straighten the loudly snoring Shlomo's covers.

Bracha was nervous and sensitive. Like every girl on the brink of adolescence, the signs of her inner disturbance were apparent on her face, which wore a sulky expression even in her sleep. And Adina, who at first had rather enjoyed the long game of hide-and-seek in the shop, and the constant presence of her parents, showed signs of anxiety after a few weeks, and as time went on her anxiety grew more acute. She was always tense, her smiles grew rare and bitter, and she often burst into tears over trifles. Sarina was worried about them both, and blamed herself and Shlomo for not succeeding in hiding their fears from the children and giving them a sense of security.

Shlomo did not trouble himself over such matters. For the most part he was sunk into himself, sighing from time to time, and to tell the truth he was only really interested in his share of the rations dished out by Sarina. But sometimes he roused himself from his apathy, and suffered attacks of keen curiosity. And it was his cross-examinations at such moments that Sarina feared above all.

In his heart of hearts Shlomo had never stopped wondering how Sarina had managed to save them at the last minute from the fate of the other Jews of Ioannina. Although he praised his wife and did not hide his admiration, there was a gleam in his eye at such moments which worried Sarina. More than once she explained (in embarrassment stemming from guilt) that she had heard suspect sounds in the neighborhood on the dawn of that fateful day, and they had roused her to take action, but it was clear that her words failed to convince her husband. Nor was he satisfied by more detailed and specific descriptions: the movement of army vehicles closing in on the neighborhood and the pasting up of notices by the Germans in the last watch of the night. In the end she called the Almighty Himself to her aid, and argued dramatically that she must have been prompted by Providence to do what she did, that a voice from heaven had irresistibly impelled her to collect food and blankets and warm clothing, to wake the sleeping members of her family and to take them to the shop.

This would silence Shlomo for a few days, after which he would break out again in a new series of questions which sounded like complaints. And who was the mysterious stranger who supplied them with food, he asked, precisely why would anyone endanger himself to help them? Someone knows that we're here, Sarina, someone who you informed of your plans – who is it? Could it be our neighbor Salima, the housepainter Aleko, or perhaps the old pharmacist Michaelides? He wondered aloud, and waited for her reply. Sarina denied everything, but was unable to find an answer that would put an end to Shlomo's questions, nor could she invent a whole new set of lies without losing her husband's trust completely.

Sometimes, when his constant questioning filled her with anger and pain and she felt she could bear it no longer, she was tempted to tell him something approaching the truth, but at the last moment she took fright and drew back. Would she have the courage to admit that she had spoken to that man in the middle of the night, that she had opened the window to the same Nazi who had come to the shop asking for names and sent her running in terror to the café? And at these moments she felt so helpless that she wanted to die. Even if the cruel conquerors tortured her like those unfortunates whose screams occasionally reached the dark interior of the shop, they wouldn't do it with such satanic slowness, feeding her their poison drop by drop, like her husband Shlomo! And sometimes she changed her mind and wondered if she wasn't tormenting herself without cause; perhaps it was only natural, understandable curiosity that was aroused in Shlomo whenever a parcel of food flew through the window and landed on the dank shop floor, and he did not suspect his wife of doing anything wrong.

Bracha and Adina, on the other hand, accepted everything with childish innocence, did not ask questions, like their father, and looked forward eagerly to the visits of the "Angel," as they called their anonymous benefactor.

One day there was a note in Hans's handwriting attached to the food parcel. Luckily Sarina noticed the note as soon as the parcel landed on the floor and she quickly hid it in her pocket. It was only a day or two later that she found an opportunity to read it. Shlomo and the girls were preoccupied by their own affairs, and the shop was momentarily illuminated by a pale ray of light. With a terrible feeling of treachery and self-hate she read the two closely written lines, in which he asked them to throw their empty water bottles out the window late at night. "Hoping you are all in good health," added Hans and signed with an illegible signature. After much thought and many doubts Sarina found a way of changing the usual routine and getting rid of the empty bottles, and things settled down again for a while. But a few weeks later Hans attached a note to the food parcel again, and this time the bag fell into the hands of

Adina, who cried excitedly to her father: "Daddy, Daddy, look, someone sent us a letter!"

When Shlomo asked to see the "letter" Sarina snatched it from her daughter's little hand and with the agility of a conjurer exchanged it for the first note, which was still hidden in her pocket.

"Nothing of importance, Shlomo," she said in a trembling voice, as if reading the crumpled note for the first time.

"The 'Angel' wants us to throw the empty water bottles out the window, and I've been doing so in any case."

Shlomo was more than usually hungry and tired that day, and his senses were dull. For otherwise, he would certainly not have passed over the incident in silence. But this time he only groaned and said, "*Kiero komer alguna koza, Sarina* (I want something to eat, Sarina)." And he looked at her imploringly.

"*Un punto* (Right away)," said Sarina and hurried to the back of the shop where she kept a few rusks for an emergency, removed them from their hiding place and gave them to Shlomo, and immediately began talking animatedly of this and that, until the note was forgotten and never mentioned again.

The second note remained buried deep in Sarina's pocket. For several days she refrained from reading it and even thought of throwing it away, as if it were the devil incarnate, but in the end she gave in. It must be something urgent, she said to herself, and my hesitations will bring a catastrophe down on my children. And she read the closely written lines. This time Hans warned them there might be a search of the shops in their street soon, and advised them to find hiding places deep in the interior of the shop, in the little gallery, or behind the bolts of cloth.

Sarina was horrified: she had wasted so much time on vain thoughts and done nothing, and every hour counted. Now she had to act at once, and if she couldn't find a convincing reason to justify her actions to Shlomo, she would simply have to put it down to a premonition that gave her no rest.

"You know, Shlomo," she began casually, "the Germans might decide any day to conduct a search of the shop. Don't you think we should find proper hiding places here, for example behind the bolts of cloth in the cupboard," she said and pointed to the back of the shop.

"*Desha, Sarina* (Leave off, Sarina)," groaned Shlomo. "If the Germans come they'll find us anyway, so why bother?"

Sarina was beside herself. For some reason she was sure that if there was a search in the shop, Hans would find a way to be present, and if the Germans didn't discover them at first glance, he would be able to lead the search party to the neighboring shops and save their lives. But how could she make Shlomo do as she wished, or, at least, prevent him from spoiling her plans?

"*Solomon kerido* (Dear Shlomo)," she turned to him at last in a tender, loving tone he had not heard from her lips in many a day, "a voice from Heaven has told me that we must do something, find a hiding place for our daughters. And if you don't want to help, then please let me do it by myself."

"Do as you wish," he replied and resumed his slumbers.

Sarina could see that Shlomo was deteriorating, growing more apathetic and weak willed from day to day, but in spite of the evidence she refused to believe it. For some months now she had seen her husband shrinking, fading in front of her eyes. The signs that had already appeared before the war were now increasingly clear, but she banished these depressing thoughts from her mind and began shifting bolts of cloth, moving chests and cupboards, padding and dusting.

She worked for hours, while Shlomo, Bracha and Adina were absorbed in their own thoughts or busy with their own affairs, and she did not rest until she had prepared a good hiding place for each of the girls. She removed the merchandise from two shelves, far apart from each other, and built up a barricade of boxes and piles of clothes to protect the person hiding behind them from the bullets of the Germans, in case they decided to shoot a few rounds during the course of their search. She asked Shlomo to go up to the gallery as soon as she gave the signal, and hide behind a screen which she had laboriously constructed in a dark corner, and behind which she had placed a comfortable chair for him to sit on. In front of the hiding place she piled up heavy bolts of cloth and all kinds of junk she found in the shop, in order to give the impression that it was a forgotten corner which nobody had visited for years.

At first she decided that she would not prepare a hiding place for herself, but that she would stand behind the counter in full view of the Germans when they came, in order to distract their attention from her family. But then she changed her mind, dismissing her original idea as silly and dangerous, and decided that when the Germans came she would kneel down and hide in the space at the bottom of the counter. In this way she would save Hans from embarrassment, if he did indeed accompany the search party, and at the same time she would be in a position to take action and try to save the day at the critical moment.

Only two untoward events took place in the shop after the second note arrived and Sarina prepared hiding places for her family. The first was the illness of Bracha, an illness whose nature Sarina did not at first comprehend and which caused her great concern. This trouble too did not arouse Shlomo from his apathy, and Sarina was obliged to cope with it herself and use her own judgement.

In the mornings Bracha would vomit, all day long she complained of pains in her stomach, and at night her forehead was burning hot. The child refused to eat, and it seemed that the danger to her life increased from day to day. There were moments when Sarina thought of leaving the shop in the dead of night and seeking help, but she kept postponing it until one morning, when she could no longer bear to see her daughter's suffering and made up her mind to set out that very night to find a doctor, she saw her weeping bitterly as she watched the blood trickling down her legs – and a weight was lifted from her heart. For hours she sat beside the girl, explaining, promising, reassuring, smiling and even laughing, but Bracha refused to be consoled. After a few days she recovered her strength and her serenity – now as a woman in every respect.

The second event that agitated and upset the already tense Sarina took place on a day in September. Another note was attached to the food parcel – the third note. This time it fell right at her feet and none of the others noticed it. "Save your food and water," it said, "we're leaving soon. And don't go outside prematurely. Love, Hans." Sarina thanked God that her daughters were not at her side. Lately – in spite of her stern warnings – they had taken to jumping up to the back window at the sound of the parcel thudding to the floor, in order to catch a glimpse of the "Angel." And once, about a week before the arrival of the third note, Adina had even cried from the heights of the shelf next to the window: "Mother! He's dressed like a German soldier. I saw him. He's a soldier. I know that he's a German soldier."

Sarina had a hard time convincing Shlomo that Adina had made the whole thing up, that her story was only a figment of the imagination of a bored child, but in the end she succeeded.

Now Sarina was beside herself, filled with anxiety by Hans's last note. For in addition to all her other worries, she now had to decide how to behave if and when the time came to leave the shop, how to explain the fact that while all the other Jews were expelled from Ioannina, she alone had known the right thing to do at the right moment in order to save her family. There was no doubt that questions would be asked, and surely Shlomo too, when he recovered from his apathy, would no longer believe her feeble excuses; he would see the connection between the "Angel," Adina's claim to have seen a German solider at the window, and his wife's "premonitions" which turned out to be so amazingly accurate. She walked around like a deaf-mute, sunk in contradictory thoughts, and for the first time since calamity had struck, she could see no solution to her dilemma. First and foremost, she worried about the fate of her daughters, but somewhere in the secret recesses of her heart, she was concerned about Hans too, and what would happen to him after he disappeared from her life.

At the beginning of October 1944 the prisoners in the shop noticed an unusual commotion outside. The noise of heavy vehicles increased from day to day. The brief commands they overheard from their hiding place sounded more impatient, less confident than usual. Sarina thought that the hour had come and that in a few days time, when quiet settled on the streets of the town, they would be able to emerge from hiding and go home. Discreetly she directed Shlomo to the proposition that all the signs pointed to the fact that the Germans had been defeated and that they were abandoning the town. In her conversations with Bracha and Adina she permitted herself to put things more clearly: "Now the wicked Germans are being punished by God," she announced, "and they're running away in a panic."

Once the belief that the siege was coming to an end had been firmly planted in the minds of Shlomo and the girls, Sarina led them to the conclusion that it was all Shlomo's idea, and she even permitted herself to disagree and offer alternative explanations for the new signs: the commotion in the streets proved nothing but the replacement of the garrison by new troops, and so on and so forth. A faint smile appeared on her lips when Shlomo scolded her and explained that the only possible explanation for the feverish activity outside was that the Germans had been defeated and had to abandon the town. He had recovered his confidence and resumed his position as the family sage, the source of authority for his wife and daughters.

Only once were the four of them seized by a great fear that their end had come. One morning a car stopped not far from the shop with a screech of brakes, a group of noisy soldiers got out, and shortly afterwards the door to the adjacent shop was broken down with a deafening crash.

"The time for looting has arrived," said Sarina, and ordered them all to conceal themselves in the hiding places she had prepared.

Luckily for them the next thing they heard was a stern command barked by an officer, and the looters returned to the vehicle. The intervals of quiet in the streets of the town grew longer, and in the shop too the silence deepened.

Patras was evacuated by the Germans at the beginning of October. Athens was liberated in the middle of the month, and the north of Greece towards its end. Refugees, victims of the persecution of the Nazi occupiers, and underground fighters gradually began returning to their homes. The few Jews who had survived the war in hiding also began emerging from their caves in the mountains, from remote villages and forests, and making their way home. Ioannina welcomed its few surviving sons.

And the survivors began to tell their hair-raising tales. Stammering, incredulous, they recounted their experiences and told of their terrible fears for the fate of their loved ones from whom they had been separated. Ioannina was no longer the same. The fate of the Jews transported to the East only became known later, when the survivors of the death camps returned and described the crematoria, the selections and the terrible suffering. The horrifying stories of the first survivor to return, Leon Biti, were at first received with scepticism, with raised eyebrows. Some even thought that Leon had lost his mind. But he gradually succeeded in persuading his audience that his words were not the deluded ramblings of a madman. Quietly, speaking in a logical, rational tone, he told of the gas chambers and the tortures undergone by the Jews of Ioannina and other Greek towns after they had been sent to Poland. And when the few other survivors arrived they added their stories to his. A black depression descended on the members of the depleted Jewish community, whose lives from now on were to be lived in the shadow of the horror. Helpless rage and a feeling of terrible betrayal filled their hearts when they realized that the world had done nothing to save them, and even friends and neighbors had not offered a helping hand.

One fine, cold morning Sarina, Shlomo, Bracha and Adina joined the hundred or so Jews who had already reached the town. The moment they raised the steel shutter was one Sarina would never forget: the glare struck them in the eyes and dazzled them for a long time. A thousand times she conjured that moment up before her and it was never enough. Again and again she remembered how she had helped Shlomo to take his first steps in the street, how she had stopped for a moment, looked straight into his indifferent eyes and ordered him, for the first time in her life, never, never to mention the "Angel" again. Where she had found the courage to do so she didn't know, but once she had done it she felt a great relief. A long-lasting anxiety vanished abruptly: let Shlomo think what he liked.

The years went by, but the shadow of the war, like the ghosts of those who had perished, continued to haunt the Jews of Ioannina, Salonika and the towns and villages of northern Greece.

Sarina continued to manage the family shop, and her duties increased from day to day. Shlomo sank into a decline. Every morning, when she raised the heavy steel shutter of the shop, she relived the terrible days she had spent in hiding with her family. And at the same time there rose before her eyes the figure of Hans knocking on her kitchen window.

One day in the summer of 1963 a group of noisy tourists arrived in the narrow street of the shops. They pushed between the stalls, looked for bargains, examined the merchandise, fingered the fabrics, compared prices, and admired the copper and leatherware handcrafted by the artists of Ioannina. The tourists, especially the Americans, made a lot of noise. A few women entered Sarina's shop while their husbands waited on the pavement outside, pestered her with questions she was already sick of answering, asked the prices of the merchandise and calculated the equivalent in dollars. One old woman with mauve hair chose two identical blouses, took out her purse and made haste to pay, as her friends told her to hurry up because the bus was about to leave for the nearby cave with the stalactites.

After the shop emptied out, Sarina addressed herself to the accounts, and every now and then she glanced out the door. Suddenly two pairs of tourists appeared, examined the scarves and belts hanging outside the shop, and spoke to each other in whispers in German. Sarina tensed. Politely but coldly she always tried to get rid of the German tourists, who had made themselves and their language so hateful to her. No, she would say to them, she did not have any more blouses and belts to choose from; no, she was not prepared to sell the bolt of cloth at a cheaper price. No, she did not accept German marks, only Greek drachmas, please.

Suddenly her heart stopped and was immediately galvanized into beating again, as if by an electric shock. The tall German tourist, with the broad, colored camera strap on his shoulder, gave her a penetrating look. He froze in his place and only his eyes darted round. He did not seem to notice that his wife and the other couple had already left the shop. Then he approached her as she stood absolutely still behind the counter, his face opposite hers, and touched her lightly on the hand gripping the edge of the counter.

"Sarina, my love," he said in English with a harsh German accent.

She stood like a marble statue and didn't move a muscle.

"Hans," she cried, but her voice was inaudible.

"Hans, Hans," the voice of his wife made itself heard and she peered into the dimness of the shop.

"*Komm schnell, der Autobus wartet nicht auf uns* (Come quickly, the bus won't wait for us)."

Hans turned on his heel. And when his tall figure disappeared, the door frame was immediately filled with the short, paunchy figure of Shlomo.

"*Otra ves los alemanes. Dio ke guadre!* (The Germans again. Heaven protect us)." Sarina stood staring and said nothing.

One year later Shlomo died.

Chapter Five

I was twenty-five years old, but it sometimes seemed to me that my father's past, which haunted me, and my own past, short but rich in the experiences of the cruel 1967 war I had survived by a miracle, had made me middle-aged. In that war Danny, my friend, had fallen right in front of me – the Jordanian Legionnaire on the Old City wall had aimed for his head and hit him right between the eyes. When I came home I clung to my father like an anxious puppy, but I only had ten more months to be with him. The night of the fire in which he perished was approaching, though I didn't know it. For about two months of the ten I served in the reserves in the "new territories." And although the remaining eight months saw my first steps on the journey of getting to know my father and coming closer to him, the time was too short for my efforts to bear fruit. Ever since then I have been continuing the journey alone, a journey into the past of a dead man.

Precisely here, in Hong Kong – God knows why – so far from home, my thoughts were troubled by the "job" I had done on my tour of duty in Gaza – a lousy job of policing, house-to-house searches, intimidation and threats. I, a combat soldier, who had always despised the "jobniks" of the Military Police and General Security Services [GSS], now found myself under their command.

"Surround the house," Yossi from the GSS commanded Giora the platoon commander. "Not a single dirty Arab goes into the yard and nobody leaves the house, not from the windows, not from the doors and not from anywhere else. Understood?" What the hell does "nobody leaves the house" mean – and what if somebody does? I asked myself, but Giora nodded obediently. What humiliation!

Rats as big and fat as the cats of Rechavia roamed the refugee camps of Jabalia and Shati with impunity, and barefoot tots with matted hair and running noses raked through the rubbish tips, some of them scavenging for scraps of food and others looking for something they could play with – a wheel, part of a machine, or an interesting-looking stick.

From these reflections I returned to the veranda of Sarina's house, which provided an excellent observation point. Previously, when I stood leaning against the railing, I had imagined taking aim at a target somewhere in the bay, and for a while I considered how I would carry out a surveillance operation from this strategic spot, how I would be able to control everything that went on in the area, with every window, every balcony and door at my command.

In Jabalia too I had quite a good observation point, even though the camp was flat. Every morning at dawn, my eyes still webbed with sleep, worn out by a long night guard duty, I would climb onto the roof of the platoon building, put my equipment down next to me, open the press studs of the canteen pouch, remove the canteen, unscrew the lid, and take a long swallow of cold water. Breakfast, I knew, was two or three hours away. Then I would take a cursory look at the inmates of the camp, my "fellow sufferers" (after all, we were all forced to be there!) – in other words the generation of the 1948 refugees and their offspring – and scan the area through the field binoculars left by my predecessor on the swollen sandbag. After satisfying myself that everything was in order, and on the assumption that there wouldn't be any "action" until everyone woke up, I would reach into the sandbags protecting the observation post and pull out a pocket book – a detective story that passed from hand to hand and shift to shift.

There is a category of "reserves literature" which you never touch from the end of one reserve duty to the beginning of the next. "Orlando whipped out his pistol. She stood facing him furiously, her breasts heaving. Slowly she went down on all fours. 'This is the last time,' he hissed between clenched teeth, 'the last time, you hear!' She nodded her head and her angry look gave way to a submissive, fawning smile…" Four pages missing, dammit. Sharvit must have ripped them out. The last person I wanted to get into an argument with. No doubt he would have them framed and hang them up in his garage office, next to the gaudy calendars and the pinups from *Playboy* magazine.

The field telephone croaks like a frog. It's Giora getting up to piss, checking to see that the guard on the roof hasn't fallen asleep. Always at the same time.

"Good morning, Giora. Everything's OK. You can go back to sleep."

"Is that you, Benny? Always the first shift, eh? Phone Operations and find out when the morning patrol goes out today. Wake me up twenty minutes after the time they tell you. OK, bye."

This conversation, which took place every morning, always coincided with the imminent emergence of the crippled child from his house, the second house on the left.

I'll never forget that child.

I went on sipping the drink Sarina's boy had given me over an hour before. And for a split second of paranoia I inspected the surface of the drink, which was unfamiliar to me, trying to ascertain if the Chinese servant had poured some exotic poison into my glass. Then I glanced at Sarina, who was absorbed in her thoughts, and returned to "my" child from Jabalia.

He would hobble between the piles of rubbish that accumulated in the camp, and I would watch him. Sometimes he would disappear behind a wall, a fence or a parked van, sometimes he would be surrounded by gangs of urchins, but he would always reappear. Now I went back and reconstructed the child's daily routine, his weekly routine, and what might turn out to be his lifelong routine. In the morning he emerged from the door of his house, in a sort of hopping crawl, and sat down on the warm sand which had already soaked up about an hour's worth of sun. Then he would begin to work on his walking apparatus – which is the only way I can define all the special means he invented and constructed so resourcefully to help himself walk. Through the binoculars I could see every detail of the child's activities, with his front door only about forty meters from the observation post. I could see it all even without the binoculars, but I felt an inexplicable, obsessive need to penetrate more deeply, to attach myself to him with the aid of the binoculars.

First he would measure a kind of artificial extension of about sixteen inches to the stump of his leg. This extension, which he had apparently made himself, was an integral part of his body, perhaps even of his very being. Afterwards he would make sure that the combined length of the stump and the improvised prosthesis was exactly equal to the length of his good leg, which he would stretch out proudly in front of him. Now it was time to attach and secure it. He would push his hand into his shirt and extract a tangled bundle of wire, and begin the delicate binding operation of attaching the prosthesis to the stump. When this stage was accomplished, he would shake his leg lightly and step on it to see if the prosthesis obeyed the commands of the stump and if the binding withstood the pressure without snapping. When he was satisfied, the faintest of smiles would appear on his lips.

From behind a whitewashed wall, which was outside my range of vision, he would deftly remove a plank and the branch of a tree. To the plank was attached a long leather strap, which he would holster onto his right shoulder, and then he would raise himself from the ground, holding tightly onto the plank, and waving the branch in his left hand. This was the signal for the stage of hopping and hobbling to begin. And thus, at a rapid limp, he would set out for his morning tour. He would begin with a thorough inspection of the rubbish bin next to the platoon building, ignoring the soldier watching him (he was so close now that I could no longer use the binoculars), and then he would vanish behind a low mound of earth and reappear with a plastic bag full of goodies – the first booty of the day.

I never saw the child's father, but I knew his brothers. I would often try to imagine the character of each one of them and their attitude towards their lame brother. I knew the mother too. She was so busy with her household chores and the needs of her children and the baby she carried in her arms that she didn't pay enough attention, in my opinion, to her disabled son, my companion.

From time to time I would talk to my father about what had happened in 1967, and of all these conversations the one that remained etched in my memory was the conversation that took place between us after I told him about an incident that occurred in the center of the town of Gaza: "One morning Giora told me to take two soldiers and go out to Medina Square. 'Your country needs you, Corporal, you weren't given those stripes for nothing,' he said sarcastically. With no choice in the matter I took the two veterans of the platoon, Sharvit and Argaman, who weren't scheduled for guard duty, we got onto the truck that brought our supplies to Jabalia, and got off in the center of town. We began patrolling the narrow alleys of the market bordering the square on foot, to 'show presence.' After about an hour an officer of the Military Government saw us as he drove past and ordered us to return to the square and climb onto the roof of the bank which overlooked the square and streets leading off it.

"'Your task is surveillance and deterrence,' he said and drove off.

"After standing there for about an hour, Sharvit and Argaman went downstairs and left me alone on the roof.

"At about four o'clock in the afternoon, while I was scanning the main street and the streets next to it for the umpteenth time through my binoculars, I saw a rusty jerrycan at the intersection of two narrow alleys next to the square. I was certain that the jerrycan had not been there the last time I checked the intersection. Again and again I inspected the suspicious object through the binoculars, and in the end I called my two partners, who climbed up to the roof unwillingly, grumbling at being interrupted in the middle of their card game.

"After inspecting the jerrycan Argaman said, 'At the most it's one more bomb, what's the big deal?'

"'You're in command of the detail,' Sharvit threw out with a sneer, 'report it to Bentzi or someone at Operations.'

"'Bullshit,' Argaman dismissed his friend's suggestion. 'Four or five dirty Arabs less, who cares. *Yallah*, let's carry on,' he turned to Sharvit and the two of them plunged into the stairwell.

"I didn't mind remaining alone with my disturbing thoughts. In any case I didn't have anything to say to those two. I had never understood them. In Jerusalem, when the fighting died down, the platoon took over the Rivoli Hotel on Salah Ed-Din

Street. And one night, when I was shift officer and I went down to check if the guards were awake, I bumped into Sharvit climbing upstairs with a huge cardboard box in his hands. 'Confiscated enemy television,' he made haste to explain.

"I learned later that he, together with Levinger, Argaman and a few more of our 'gallant warriors' had broken into Arab shops and helped themselves to whatever they could lay their hands on. Only then did I realize why, for the first time in my career as platoon sergeant, I had had no difficulty in organizing guard duty at night; the exhausting arguments about justice and fairness had evaporated into thin air. And now, even though Sharvit was stronger, more violent and also much older than I was (he had been serving in the regiment since the War of Independence), I barred his way and informed him unequivocally that if he did not return the 'looted items' – for some reason, those were the words I used – I would report him to the guys in the Ambassador Hotel, in other words, the MPs.

"He was furious. 'I'll get you for this,' he spat out and banged the television set down on the stairs. 'Go on, go and return the "looted items" to your buddies you love so much.' And still beside himself with rage, he came right up to me, grabbed hold of my shirt, and with his eyes flashing and boring into mine, he promised me that 'before the war was over' he would settle his score with me. After that he and his mates never stopped mocking me and telling anyone prepared to listen that I had caused them 'serious financial damage.'"

In that conversation with my father I brought up the subject of the suspect jerrycan at the crossroad in Gaza. I told him what had happened and asked him, "What would you have done in my place?"

It was evident from my father's face that the situation was alien to him, and he was even embarrassed when he saw that I was waiting for his answer. He was never really a military man; he had only served briefly in the IDF and that at a time when regular army procedures had not yet been fully established. My father sank into a reverie and I did not press him. It seemed to me that he had lost his sensitivity to many things a long time ago, at an early stage of his life, when he was still in Ioannina.

As a father, he had mixed feelings about my inner "seismograph." On the one hand, he applauded my human sensitivity, and on the other hand he was not sure I was directing it towards the right objects. During our conversations he seemed conscious both of the common ground between us and of the different paths we had taken, which had led us further away from each other. Sometimes it seemed to me that he would have preferred me to pay more attention to what he called the "wider historical contexts" – national, regional and international – and concern myself less with the "trivia" of the "local and immediate," which seemed to him essentially personal and therefore marginal and of secondary importance. It was clear to me that he had nothing to the point to say about my story up to now, and that in the depths of his heart he considered it a waste of time to pay too much attention to transient episodes and to look for any great significance in them.

"Never mind, Father," I said to put an end to the embarrassing silence, "I'll just tell you quickly what happened afterwards. I called Bentzi on the radio. He came in a jeep with another few functionaries from Operations. They looked at the jerrycan, but kept a safe distance away. They weren't demolition experts and had no desire to fiddle with a suspicious object. After they conferred between themselves Bentzi reported the problem to the Military Government office and a tough-looking dark-haired lieutenant finally drove up in a gleaming new jeep, the likes of which you would never find in a field platoon, but it immediately transpired that he too was afraid to touch the jerrycan. He looked around at a loss, barking a few brief commands to hide his embarrassment. He stood next to the radio in his jeep for about ten minutes, but was apparently unable to obtain precise instructions or to get hold of a demolitions squad. In the meantime the passersby began to take an interest in the unusual activity at the crossroads. Some of them looked into the eyes of the Israeli soldiers as if trying to get to the bottom of the problem. You have to understand, Father, at that stage the idea of a terrorist bomb at such a busy Arab center still seemed inconceivable to most people.

"Bentzi and the lieutenant didn't evacuate the inhabitants from the danger area. And then something happened that to me is a landmark. The lieutenant suddenly recovered and ordered one of the bystanders in Arabic to go up to the jerrycan and lift it in both hands, and then pointed to an empty field on the other side of the road as if indicating that he should throw the jerrycan there. The Arab to whom the lot had fallen, a young man in jeans and sneakers, shrugged his shoulders and with an aggressive gesture refused to obey the order. The lieutenant went up to him and a fight immediately broke out between them. Our soldiers separated them and stood the Arab youth against the jeep with his hands on the tarpaulin roof. He kept up a steady stream of protests and from time to time he tried to use his hands to make himself clear. But in vain. Every time he tried to turn his head or point at the jerrycan, somebody stopped him and prevented him from taking his hands off the tarpaulin.

"By now it was already clear to everybody why the Jewish soldiers and the two officers were standing at the street corner. From the roof of the building I saw how the news spread through the square, and how the passersby went out of their way to circumvent the danger spot. The lieutenant's mission now became much harder to carry out. Everyone began slowly and nonchalantly moving away, and the lieutenant was forced to look for his victims in an ever-widening circle. The numbers of those with their hands on the roof of the jeep grew from minute to minute and the jeep was already surrounded on all sides, like the altar in some strange ritual ceremony. Gradually the voices died down and a great silence descended, an ominous silence. I thought: in another minute there'll be an explosion here which will be a lot worse than the explosion of a jerrycan. They're quite likely to fall on the soldiers and lynch them. The lieutenant was red in the face with rage. He barked orders at our soldiers in Hebrew, and cursed the detainees in Arabic. Bentzi was at a loss. He simply didn't know what to do. He didn't like the whole business. I knew him – we'd been serving together in the regiment for a long time. He tried to remain on the sidelines as if the whole thing had nothing to do with him.

"And you know what happened in the end, Father? The lieutenant suddenly broke through the circle formed by the parked vehicles and the soldiers standing between them, crossed the road with a determined air, grabbed hold of a little boy standing there by himself and staring into space, dragged him by the arm into the middle of the circle and yelled at him like a wild animal. The child rushed frantically up to the jerrycan, picked it up in both hands and raced to the open field. At a distance of a few meters from the edge of the field he stopped and threw the jerrycan at a rock covered with yellow thorns in the middle of the field. There was a hollow sound and the jerrycan rolled over twice and landed quietly on its side. The eerie silence was broken. The large crowd seemed to breathe a sigh of relief in unison and began to disperse. With the swagger of a national hero the lieutenant went up to the jerrycan, picked it up and examined it, peered inside it and lifted it into the air as if it was the head of the slain Goliath, and then, like a phony David, he looked at the camp of the Israelites with a silly grin on his face.

"Suddenly a woman's scream rose from the crowd returning to its daily routine, a terrible scream I shall never forget as long as I live. A peasant woman in a black embroidered dress rushed up to the child, who was now standing not far from the jeep, clasped him in her arms, kissed him, and then raised both arms in the air and cried: '*Bigi yomo, ibni, bigi yomo!* (His day will come, my son, his day will come!)' And I felt my eyes filling with tears. Yes, for the first time since I was a child, I wept.

"Life in the square returned to normal. The soldiers dispersed. Sharvit and Argaman came up to the roof. 'Did something happen?' asked Sharvit. 'What about the jerrycan?' inquired Argaman. 'Someone removed it,' I replied, and wiped away a tear with my sleeve as if it was an annoying drop of sweat. 'Go and rest, we'll take over for a bit,' they said."

I had concluded my story. My father's face remained inscrutable.

I returned to the remote and exotic world of the colony and through the mists of time and space I heard Sarina's voice, "*Benazariko, kieres komer alguna koza?* (Benazariko, do you want to eat something?)"

"*Grasias munchas, no* (Thank you very much, no)."

"I'm going out to do a few things. I'll be back soon."

I wanted to be by myself for a while. In the distance I heard the sound of my aunt's high heels. The boy came out to the veranda and took the empty glass, which I had put down on the little table. He had a yellow duster in his hand and a feather duster under his arm. And then I saw again that he didn't walk on the veranda floor like an ordinary mortal, but seemed to hover a few inches above it, like a hovercraft. His movements were those of a being from another world – quick, efficient, and unexpected. The look he gave me out of the corner of his slanting eyes was strange too. Was he watching me – as a supervisor or a spy? Or perhaps he was afraid I would turn into a dragon and swallow him up? And I, even though I had always sneered at the uncanny and the supernatural, shifted uneasily in my chair.

"Kalamaro," I whispered, "Kalamaro."

Did I do it to provoke the boy, or did I perhaps see it as a magic formula intended to bring me back from the strange world in which I found myself to the world of reality? I didn't know. But I knew very well that the Chinese servant had flown away and disappeared, and the glass that had been at my side before was no longer there. I had no doubt that his appearance had been an illusion.

In a weak voice I hummed my private song about Kalamaro from Arlozorov Street to myself.

Kalamaro had a white suit and white shoes. His hair and his glasses too were speckled with white. On Saturday afternoons he would stand, tall and thin, on the corner of Azza and Arlozorov Streets. He didn't belong to any generation, to any framework; he was an independent entity. For hours he would stand staring into space, and then he would begin gliding weightlessly down Arlozorov Street in the direction of the Salvia Hotel.

Suddenly I knew: Kalamaro and the Chinese boy were one and the same, even though Kalamaro was alive and kicking in Jerusalem (I had seen him there before I left Israel). It's a well-known fact that the transmigration of souls does not recognize the boundaries between the world of the dead and the world of the living, but there was apparently also a geographical transmigration of the soul, from continent to continent, from place to place. And I had just discovered it!

"In Jerusalem," Kalamaro would say, "the gutters are always dripping – in the winter rainwater and in the summer water from the old tanks on the roofs. These tanks are either on the point of overflowing or else they've already overflowed. Can you imagine what pressures the Jerusalem tanks have to withstand? They're always full of water, year in year out, and the internal pressure is immense. And suddenly the ball cock doesn't work, the metal gradually rusts away and the grooves deepen. In most of the buildings in Jerusalem the water flows from the tank for a week or two and sometimes longer, until someone notices and takes the trouble to go up to the roof. Then comes the repair, which is always a patchwork affair, and then it's the turn of the neighbor's tank to overflow. And so on and so forth."

I surveyed the view of the roofs in front of me and I saw that here in the colony there were no water tanks at all.

Amina, my mother's aunt, was married to Kalamaro. They were childless. Amina died on the 29th of November 1947, just before the United Nations resolution on Partition was announced, and when everyone was dancing in the streets Kalamaro sat alone in his grief. The sight of the joyful celebrations while his own heart was aching was unbearable to him, and even many years later he was still brooding over it.

One day he invited me to the Azza Café. We had met by chance on Azza Street and he didn't want to let me go. He talked and talked and I felt that I couldn't leave him by himself. In the café, as we drank our lemon tea, he finally fell silent. And then he whispered confidentially, "Aunt Amina is sick, very sick." I was shocked – Aunt Amina had been buried on the Mount of Olives for nearly twenty years. But I only said that I was very sorry to hear it. I knew that for Kalamaro everything had frozen on the day the British left the country. On no account could he adjust to the new reality, to the existence of an independent Jewish state in the Land of Israel.

"With the British," this fan of the Mandate would open every second sentence, "such things couldn't happen, believe me." And he would immediately begin to list all the evils that had overtaken us since the last British soldier had left the country: income tax, the shortcomings of public institutions and bureaucratic procedures, and so on and so forth. "You know what they did to a civil servant who came late for work under the British? And today I saw a clerk in the Rechavia Post Office sitting behind the counter in a grey undershirt, his mouth full of a sandwich, drinking tea and talking on the phone while customers were waiting. You hear? I saw it with my own eyes!"

About relations between Jews and Arabs after the War of Independence he spoke with anger. "Look, on the whole we lived in peace with the Arabs. Yes, I'm telling you, there was peace, there was order, and economic prosperity too. What did we lack?" The disturbances of 1929 and 1936–37 he dismissed with a wave of his hand. In his eyes these were no more than transient episodes, the products of coincidence, and not clashes stemming from contradictions between the character and aspirations of the Jewish and Arab populations.

To reinforce his arguments he would admiringly describe the atmosphere in Barclays Bank in Jaffa Street during the Mandate: "The way they treated customers then! And now?! It's all backbiting and petty politics! Do you read the newspapers, Benhazar? Do you know what's going on here? We have to bring back the British. Yes, we have to bring them back. I know what you think: 'Independence is important, people have to fight for their motherland, freedom or death.' Yes, yes, I know, but let me tell you, my young friend, that in other British colonies too, ex-colonies of course, people are dying for them to come back. I just received a letter from Malaya, from a friend of mine, an Indian from Malaya. He was here in the thirties. We would sit in the King David Hotel together for hours on end, drinking and talking. I never had a friend like him before or since. And what does he write? He had a business there, a flourishing business. The British left, and now he's crying out to high heaven. Corruption, dirty politics, strife and rottenness. That's what they've got in Malaya now. In India too there's a lot of discontent. Look at the trouble they're in now that Nehru's gone. Tell me, was Lord Mountbatten so bad?"

And then, after a long silence Kalamaro would begin to attack Jochanan: "Don't let your father influence you too much. He's a good man, I respect and value him. He's a clever man. He's done a lot for the nation. All right, granted, but that anti-British insanity of his drove him out of his mind, not to mention that business with the Japanese."

In those days I didn't pay too much attention to his words, but now I tried to remember them in detail. There was more than a hint at the subject that was now uppermost in my mind, but despite my efforts I was unable to remember more than the phrase "that business with the Japanese," accompanied by the turning of his index finger on his temple.

Suddenly I shook off these thoughts and memories and rose resolutely to my feet, left the veranda, crossed the living room and slipped out of the house without saying anything to the boy, who was busy dusting the stuffed-bird cupboard while muttering unintelligibly to himself.

In Connaught Street, in the center of the colony in a highrise building, was the office of Mr. George Woodhead, whose name had been mentioned in passing by Major Holmes before he stormed angrily out of the room when I met him in Oxford. I wanted to speak to him about my father, because I believed that he was in possession of important information about his activities. During the taxi journey and the long ascent in the elevator I racked my brains unsuccessfully for a gambit with which I could approach Mr. Woodhead. And as I crossed the spacious lobby with its dark-brown wood-panelled walls, and approached the secretary's office, it was already too late to find one. She raised her head and examined me with her slanting eyes, glittering with a beauty from another world.

When she heard my request she sighed politely, "I'm very sorry. Without an appointment in advance I won't be able to let you in to see him."

"I…"

"I'm very sorry. Mr. Woodhead is very busy. Even if you ask for an interview you won't get one until the end of the month."

I stood there without budging in spite of my embarrassment. Was this the bureaucratic rigidity that had so endeared the British to Kalamaro? I asked myself. And I muttered, as much to myself as to her, "I have to see Mr. Woodhead today."

For a moment the secretary fixed me with her beautiful eyes and then she immediately returned to her work.

Woodhead was the director of a large marketing company. During the war he had been regarded as close to the Chinese – both to the Communists and Chiang Kai-shek's men – and he had performed various missions for British intelligence in the Far East. He became known as a shrewd and daring fighter, who acted behind the lines of the Japanese enemy in China and other places in Southeast Asia, and many legends grew up around his exploits. Nobody could understand how he had emerged safe and sound from the cruel and complicated war in which he had played such a dangerous role. His figure engaged both journalists and novelists after the war, and one popular spy story referred to his activities in quite a detailed way. But after the war he devoted himself to his business affairs and apparently erased every trace of his former life. "Don't expect him to talk to you about the war," Major Holmes had warned me in Oxford.

I seated myself on the comfortable sofa opposite the secretary's desk, leafed through a magazine that was lying on the table in front of me and thought about what to do next. I decided not to budge until Mr. Woodhead agreed to see me. "Let's see who gets tired first," I said to myself, and from time to time I glanced at the well-groomed Chinese woman, who pretended to be oblivious of my annoying presence. Her nails were painted a gleaming dark red, and her sensuous lips were red too. Gradually I realized that I was devoting more and more attention to her. Her breasts were small, almost flat, but my eyes were drawn to the crossed legs extending from her short skirt. A desirable woman, I summed up to myself, as her slender fingers danced with lightning speed over the keys of her electric typewriter. Her stylish glasses were perched with casual elegance on the tip of her nose. And again I dropped my eyes to her legs and the stiletto heels of her shoes.

The telephone rang and she said a few words in a clipped guttural drone and put the receiver down. It rang again and this time she contented herself with a brief "Thank you." For a couple of hours she never moved from her desk, working diligently without a break. When she finished typing the letters she began writing in her notebook. Again and again she answered the phone, without wasting words, without going into unnecessary details – everything was cold, brisk, correct and precise. Yes, this was the way people were supposed to work, this was British discipline, but where was the heart, where was the warmth, the humanity?

I leaned my head against the back of the sofa and sailed far away to the butterfly collection in Beth Hakerem, to Ilana Hamburger and the old woman with the shopping baskets in the wadi, and a tremor ran through my body. Once more I saw Ilana and the old lady trying to revive me and whispering to each other, I smelled the ammonia and the eau-de-cologne, I tasted the cold, honey-sweet drink set to my lips. And then I opened my eyes and saw the Chinese secretary bending over me solicitously: with a practised hand she removed a cloth steeped in an intoxicating aroma from my forehead, and for the first time a broad smile spread over her face as she saw me open my eyes. But I immediately plunged back into the dark abyss, sliding down on the sofa. Again I tried to open my eyes. The room was dark and there was not a sound to be heard. I was hot. The secretary removed her blouse and her little breasts stood erect. Who said that the Chinese were yellow? They were brown. She bent over me and I sank into sleep.

The next day I found myself sitting in a leather armchair opposite the stern-faced Mr. Woodhead. Only once during the interview the Chinese secretary came into the room, whispered something to her boss, and ignored my presence.

"I have no interest in exposing confidential, hitherto unknown, details about the way the British conducted the war in this region," I began. "I only want one thing from you. You must have heard about my father, Jochanan Cohen, John Cohen, or simply J.C. He died in a terrible accident in Jerusalem. And I, his son, would like to know about his activities in this region during the war, about his contacts with the Japanese, for the sake of which he disappeared from Palestine during the years in question. I would be grateful if you could tell me what he was up to here, in Burma and in New Delhi?"

Woodhead shifted in his chair. "I've made it a rule not to talk to anyone about secret matters related to the war. I'm a practical man – let the journalists and historians burrow in the documents or interview the chatterboxes and publicity hounds. I've turned over that page in my life. But this time I'm prepared to make an exception, since this is a family matter, and tell you what I know about your father." And after a short, hesitant silence he muttered, "I can't refuse Leonardo Reil. I'd do a lot for him."

I didn't understand what my meeting with Woodhead had to do with Leonardo. Had I said something to Sarina about wanting to speak to him? But I immediately dismissed these speculations from my mind and pricked up my ears.

"Mr. Cohen," Woodhead began in a slightly formal tone, as if opening a meeting, "your father, who adopted many different underground names, was a member of the Stern Gang, and if he imagined that we, even in this distant theater of the war, didn't know about his activities, he must have been incredibly naive. Yes, I really think that in spite of the impossible missions he carried out, in spite of his clandestine activities, he was as naive as a child, incorrigibly naive.

"He arrived in Hong Kong two or three weeks before the attack on Pearl Harbor and before our colony fell to the Japanese. We felt then that our fate was sealed. Although the Americans were taken by surprise by the attack on Pearl Harbor, we over here expected it. We simply knew the Japs better than they did; we were familiar with their cruelty, their viciousness and their dirty tricks. After the atrocities they committed in Nanking – the brutal rapes and murders – nothing they did could surprise us. You people, in Europe and Palestine, go on about the crimes of the Nazis. Yes, when it comes to the murder of Jews you deafen heaven and earth with your cries, but the holocausts of other nations are very quickly forgotten. Can you even imagine what the Chinese suffered in the long years of the war? Let's ignore the immense numbers of the victims for the moment – more than the Jews exterminated by the Nazis, by the way – but did you know that in some parts of China starvation was so severe that there were instances of cannibalism? Can you imagine what happened when the Chinese capital fell in December 1937 and eighty thousand Japanese rampaged through the city for days on end, raping more than twenty thousand women and murdering two hundred thousand people in cold blood? We lived the cruelty of the Japanese every day.

"And then your father arrived. In my opinion he chose Hong Kong because the atmosphere here was more conducive to making connections with the Japanese intelligence community than in Tokyo. Or so he thought at least. If he had gone straight to Tokyo from British Palestine, he would have been suspected and thrown into jail. Why he came to me, I don't know. Perhaps precisely because he knew what my role and connections were he wanted to pull the wool over my eyes and appear innocent and harmless. And perhaps he thought he would be able to get some information he needed out of me. To this day there are things that aren't clear to me.

"One day I found your father waiting in my office. When I discovered that the man standing in front of me was none other than Jochanan Cohen I was astounded. After exchanging a few civilities, he told me that he was interested in Japanese history and culture. Yes, bloody Japanese culture if you don't mind. You must understand, Mr. Cohen, that in those days Japanese culture meant to me a 'culture' of murder and rape. The events of those years had wiped out everything I knew and everything

I had admired up to then in the culture of the Japanese. In my youth I read about the foreign penetration of Japan, about the 1853 ultimatum delivered to that peaceful people by the American Commodore Perry, and I had also read the works of George Sansom, who had served in the British embassy in Tokyo as an advisor in the thirties and who was a great expert on Japan. And precisely he favored dealing harshly with the Japanese militarists, who were sprouting then like weeds, and was horrified when he realized to what lengths of insanity the Japanese were being led by their history.

"But to return to your father, young Mr. Cohen. Your father asked me to help him make contact with Japanese academics and intellectuals in Hong Kong. The irony of fate: in order to become acquainted with the treasures of Japanese culture your father needed a favor from the cruel "British brutes" he was fighting in Palestine. And as he sat opposite me in my office I had his file in front of me. He held forth in an elevated tone about spiritual and cultural matters, and all the time I was thinking about the reports on his extreme political views and the atrocities attributed to him and his friends in Palestine. Our men in the Middle East had done a first-class job. There were even photographs of him in various disguises lying in front of me. What did he think, that he would be able to lead us by the nose?

"You know, young Mr. Cohen, there were moments during that conversation with your father when I simply wanted to hand him the file lying in front of me. If I had been a free agent I might even have done it. And what satisfaction it would have given me! But I had been given explicit instructions not to stop him and to let him go on playing his game. Our people wanted to know exactly what he was up to. Was it a private initiative, or had his organization decided to extend their contacts with the Fascists and Nazis in Europe to collaboration with Tokyo too? The whole thing was insane, even in terms of the general insanity of the war. An intellectual, a historian – what in God's name did he think he was doing?"

Woodhead was obviously upset and agitated. The thought flashed through my mind that up to this moment he had repressed his memories of the war and refused to talk about it not for the reasons he gave, but because he was afraid of losing control of himself. He was apparently not as strong a man as he seemed on the surface. And nevertheless, in his own way he appeared to enjoy this unexpected meeting with the son of Jochanan Cohen. For him it was simply a continuation of the conversation he had been forced to cut short with my father. Everything he was forbidden to say then, in November 1941, he spoke of now, twenty-seven years later, almost without inhibition.

"I let your father play his game. I directed him to a few Japanese who were living here then – Japanese who needless to say were collaborating with us," he added proudly, "and a few minutes after every conversation he had with them we knew exactly what had been said. Forgive me for saying so, but your father was an extremist, a fanatic who knew no limits. And at the same time incredibly naive, a real crank. Do you know what he wanted? He believed that since the Japs were anti-British and had begun acting to liquidate the European colonies in Asia, including the strategic assets so important to us, the Jewish national movement had to join hands with the liberating Japanese. They would be the friends of the Jewish people! To this very day I can't understand how anyone could entertain such a nonsensical plan. Did he think the Japs were any better than the Nazis? Do you know what they did to our POWs here in the East? Can you imagine what those ugly dwarfs would have done to you if they had ever reached Palestine and their German allies had asked them to?"

Woodhead fell silent, took a sip of water from the glass before him, breathed in deeply, and went on talking with forced composure. He was evidently determined not to let himself be carried away by his emotions.

"Your father's file swelled from day to day. We waited for orders to arrest him. We had become increasingly convinced that he was acting on his own. That his comrades in arms over there, in Palestine, had hardly any connection to his operation and perhaps they didn't know anything about it. There was no point in waiting any longer, but I couldn't act without orders. He was pinning down manpower and resources that we needed for other, more important matters in those critical days. But the order didn't come. Someone in London thought we should accede to the request of the authorities in Palestine and see the operation through to the end. And one day he simply disappeared, vanished from the face of the earth as if it had opened up and swallowed him. We were obliged to allocate even more resources to chasing after this crank. Our intelligence community was in a turmoil, as if there wasn't a war going on in our region, and the wave of mutual recriminations swelled – but I won't bore you with the details, Mr. Cohen."

For the first time since I had entered his office Woodhead smiled, and sank into his thoughts.

"You know," he said in the end, "perhaps your father, for all his naivety and eccentricity, succeeded in tricking us. He took his revenge in his own unique and crazy way. Be that as it may, a few days later the Japanese beast attacked us."

Woodhead described the suffering to which Europeans were subjected then all over Asia, dwelling especially on the plight of the British in the Japanese "Stanley" prison camp in

Hong Kong. About himself he said nothing, apart from hinting that with the help of underground forces operating in occupied China he had succeeded in escaping from the colony. It was possible to guess that he had been delegated to carry out various clandestine operations in the region – the source of the many legends associated with his name. Two years later he arrived in New Delhi and joined his colleagues in the British intelligence community there.

"In the spring of 1944 we received jumbled reports from behind enemy lines concerning the presence of an eccentric white man at Subhas Chandra Bose's headquarters in Japanese-occupied Burma, or to be more precise, in Maimio next to Mandalay. Although there were occasional cases of Europeans – even Englishmen, to my shame – who collaborated with the Japanese, it was clear that this was a special case. We knew for certain that the man wasn't a German, and when we tried to find out who he was and where he came from, we discovered that his English was seasoned with Spanish. We couldn't fit him into any logical framework and we referred to him simply as "Mister X." We had a junior officer on our staff, a bright young Scot, who specialized in solving mysteries of this kind. He studied documents and files that had accumulated since the beginning of the war and finally reached the conclusion that the man we were looking for was Jochanan Cohen – J.C., as he was referred to in our documents. I remember that none of us were prepared to accept this conclusion. To the extent that we had the time to think about J.C. at all, we assumed that he had returned clandestinely to Palestine to join his underground comrades there.

"In the summer after the Kohima and Imphal campaigns we came into possession of some papers from one of the Japanese commands. They confirmed the young Scot's hypothesis that the strange white man who had joined the Japanese forces was indeed J.C. We realized that far from abandoning his fantastic dream, the expansion of the war had only made him more determined to carry it out, as we learned from an internal memo signed by a political officer in the Japanese command. Until the turning point at El Alamein and the news of the extermination of the Jews, he still expected, like some of his fellows in the Stern Gang, that the Germans and Italians would conquer West Asia and Palestine, while the Japanese liberated the peoples of the rest of Asia from the imperialist yoke. This was the course which the anti-imperialist struggle was supposed to take. When the plan went wrong, and the tide turned against the Germans in Europe and North Africa, J.C. went on hoping that the Japanese would complete the work of liberation on their own. He believed that the Japanese, whose momentum, at least on land, had not been checked, would continue to fulfill their 'historic mission.'

"Only in the summer of 1944, with the defeat of their forces and their retreat from Imphal, did your father give up his dream. We went on looking for him, but of course we had more urgent and important things to do. Your father, with all the professional respect we had for him as a gifted amateur, was not our top priority. Before the end of the war I left Asia. My connections with my colleagues were broken off. About a year after the war I was told that your father had been traced to Jerusalem, after which he disappeared again, as usual, without leaving a trace.

"That's it, my young friend. For twenty-two years I haven't given the man a thought, and now you, his son, are sitting here in front of me. The circle is closed. I sympathize with you on the loss of your father. He was a strange man, a stranger wherever he went. I only hope that he found peace at the end."

With this Woodhead said goodbye to me, after promising that on one of his frequent trips to England he would pay a flying visit to Israel. "I have to see what you Jews have done there with my own eyes."

I left feeling drained, with my mind in a turmoil. I missed my father, the "grey" man from Rutenberg Lane, intensely. For hours I roamed the streets of the colony. I made my way between the stalls of people selling all kinds of exotic fish, snakes and crustaceans, hearing the heavy Cantonese dialect on all sides without taking anything in. In the end I took the ferry across the straits to Kowloon, hired a taxi and drove around the "new territories," in a landscape more foreign than anything I had ever seen in my life. And whenever my eyes fell on some shrine or temple, some green field or beautiful Hakka girl in a broad-brimmed hat trimmed with black lace, I asked myself, did my father see this too? Did he too drive down this road, see this hut? But for the driver, who took me back to the ferry station when evening fell on his own initiative, I would no doubt have gone on driving around for hours.

When I returned home Sarina greeted me with questions that revealed her anxiety: "*Ke paso, kerido mio? Es ke stas hazino?* (What happened, my dear? Are you ill?)"

"*No, tia kerida, sto kansado, kiero dormir* (No, dear aunt, I'm tired. I want to sleep)."

I begged her pardon, retired to my room and fell into bed, and a few seconds later I was sound asleep.

Chapter Six

Nobody mentioned my mother, I said to myself as the wheels hit the runway at Lydda airport. On all my previous trips abroad I had felt a thrill when the plane landed in Israel, but not this time. Had I become jaded? Perhaps at the entrance to Jerusalem I would sense the old happiness and elation, the acceleration of my heartbeat as the taxi drove down Jaffa Street? And again I said to myself: nobody mentioned my mother.

At the outskirts of Romema, on the left of the road, stands the Sephardi old-age home – not "retirement home," not "parents' home," not "senior citizens' residence," but simply old-age home. This was where my grandfather's brother lived. On Sabbath eves and religious holidays my father would visit his uncle and take him an "offering," as for some reason he called the bag of spinach and cheese burekas and sweetmeats. I would often accompany him on these visits. We would find Grandpa, as I called my great-uncle, sitting in the hallway wearing a fez. Long after he abandoned the striped galabiyeh and exchanged it for a "European" suit, he went on clinging to this red Turkish hat. For hours on end he would sit with his fellow inmates on the benches lining the hallway leading into the rooms and stare into space. When we approached he would smile. I would bow my head and he would bless me with his trembling hands and kiss me. Then my father would begin talking to him in Ladino, a language he rarely used, but which dominated the old-age home as if it had been transported here together with the inhabitants directly from Ottoman Salonika. It was a language of suffering and pain. The revived Hebrew language was set aside for free and easy chatter, full of life and youthful laughter, while the Jewish Spanish was left with the anxiety and the sorrow.

When I was about six my great-uncle died. He was not buried in the plot he had purchased on the Mount of Olives, because as soon as the War of Independence broke out the road there was cut off, and instead of burying him in the ground hurriedly consecrated on the hill of Sheik Badar for the Jewish dead of the town, his body was interred on the edge of the field next to the Shaare Zedek Hospital. This great privilege was granted by Dr. Wallach, the charismatic hospital manager, to only a select few of his intimate friends, those who worshipped with him at the hospital synagogue, and my great-uncle was among them. He whispered this promise into the ear of each one of his favorites, in order not to give rise to jealousy, like some great monarch promising a faithful knight a fief in perpetuity, for him and his sons after him.

Back in Jerusalem again after my long absence abroad, I remembered the stories told in the family about the doctor's cruelty to patients in need of his help on the Sabbath. When one of my relations suffered a sunstroke on the Sabbath, while sitting outside his house next to the sundial, not far from the hospital, the doctor refused to come, and when he did come, at the end of the Sabbath, it was already too late. Only a miracle saved the good doctor from being lynched by the family and neighbors.

The newspaper *Haheruth* (Liberty) from the year 1913 reported a similar incident which took place a few years previously: an ultra-Orthodox Jew, a builder called Moshe Dov Berger from Jaffa, who traveled to Jerusalem with his sick son Shmuel on a Saturday and brought him straight to the Shaarei

CHAPTER SIX

Tzedek Hospital, was cursed for desecrating the Sabbath and thrown out bodily by the esteemed doctor himself, and the sick boy lay in Jaffa Street outside the hospital gates until eight o'clock in the evening, and died the next day. "For the past ten years this savage doctor has headed the most important Hebrew institution in the country, and during that time he has accustomed the residents of Jerusalem to his pious virtues: to beat and curse his patients, to force the gravely ill to rise from their beds in order to pray. There is a limit to everything," the newspaper argued, "even in the wild and desolate wastes of Jerusalem," and demanded the resignation of Dr. Wallach from his post.

If anyone checked it out, I said to myself, they would discover that what all those privileged to be buried in the yard of Dr. Wallach's hospital had in common was the fact that they were all witnesses to the murder of Dr. Jacob de Haan, who opposed the idea of the national home and the Balfour Declaration, by a Haganah member outside the green gate at the corner of the hospital wall on June 30, 1924, while they were at their prayers. This murder made it clear to any of the worshippers who still needed a clarification (as Grandpa repeatedly stressed), that nobody knew when he would be called to meet his Maker, for there was only a hair's breadth between his grey head and the bullet that had felled the victim. And for some reason I kept on imagining Grandpa standing at the little green gate, dismayed and bewildered, with the murdered man bleeding at his feet.

Two or three times a year my father would visit his uncle's grave. He would usually take me with him, and we would stand there together. My father would stand in silence, sunk in thought. He never whispered a prayer, but I had no doubt that he was wandering in other worlds. I would look at him and wait, and when I got bored I would read the words engraved on Grandpa's tombstone over and over again (sometimes in reverse order), as if seeking a clue to some sublime mystery in them. His figure would slowly rise before my eyes, familiar but at the same time slightly different. Then I would slide my eyes cautiously over the tombstones next to his, trying to attach the names on them to the faces of the friends who used to sit in the passage of the old-age home with him, staring into space. When my father came back to earth he would shake himself and begin walking slowly between the neglected tombstones (some of them looked as if they were turning on an invisible hinge, as if the inhabitants had gone out for a short walk and absentmindedly forgotten to close the marble door behind them) with me behind him, and we would wander there as if in search of something beyond our grasp.

We always entered the little graveyard through a gap in the fence, opposite the prefabs that would one day house the Foreign Ministry, and leave through the same gap. On the way home my father would hasten his steps, and I would run panting to keep up with him, afraid that if I fell behind he would leave me there alone in the deserted streets, prey to the spirits of the dead who had not found their way to their resting place. My father would choose a winding path through the houses of Nachlaot, as if he too wanted to pull the wool over the eyes of the threatening ghosts, and I would rack my brains for a way to attract his attention and make him slow down (shout? fall? beg?). Thus we would arrive at Ussishkin Street leading to Rechavia. Here my father would shorten his steps, ready to keep pace with me, and perhaps even to talk to me. But I knew that I had better keep quiet and wait until we reached the Evelina de Rothschild School and the Sephardi synagogue on its grounds. For here, experience had taught me, my father would utter his first sentence, as a sign that the memorial rites for Grandpa were over.

Aunt Flora, my father's aunt on his mother's side, who lived at the bottom of Ussishkin Street, always caught us on the way back from the cemetery. After much thought, I came up with two possible explanations for this, one of which had to be right: either she spent all her time sitting on the balcony of her apartment, or else she was endowed with a supernatural sense by means of which, like some sophisticated instrument not yet invented by the Americans or their Russian opponents, she was able to keep invisible moves and events under surveillance and know many things – such as the exact moment when my father and I would pass her house.

"*Ven aki* (Come here)," Aunt Flora would call to my father. And to me she would say, "*Benazariko kerido, tengo un konfit para ti* (Benazariko my dear, I have a sweet for you)." And for fear I would not understand her Ladino, she would add, "*Sukariotes, sukariotes* (Candies, candies)."

My father would look at me with an expression whose meaning never became clear to me, and we would go inside. I would sit down on the angular chair upholstered in brown leather with white cracks which multiplied as the years went by, dreading the ghastly boredom in store for me. The conversations in Ladino between my father and Aunt Flora were like a nightmare. After a few civilities about the health of the family, she would begin to complain about the depression that had her in its grip – the famous *strechura* – and list all kinds of troubles and problems that were remote and alien to me then – although today I think that I would have found her stories interesting and I might have learned a lot from them. The *sukariotes* she offered me to the accompaniment of warm, wet kisses were not to my taste, and the lemonade was sour and disgusting. I would therefore withdraw into myself and sail away on the wings of my imagination.

First I would imagine that the chair on which I was sitting was standing above the entrance to an empty tunnel which I would be able to enter after removing the lid of tiles covering it. Then I would see myself in my mind's eye descending into the mysterious tunnel, through the middle of which ran a narrow railway track with an express car that would take me straight to the Valley of the Cross, and there, not far from the "Little Acorn," I would meet my friends Gershon, Menashe, Shlomo, Moshe and Oded, and ramble with them though the grass and flowers of the valley. And when some technical difficulty got in my way (how, for instance, would I be able to breathe in the long tunnel?) I would immediately come up with a plan to circumvent it: I would see myself taking a tiny balloon out of my pocket and with a couple of magic puffs turning it into a gas balloon that would carry me through the big window of Aunt Flora's apartment into the wide blue sky. With scrupulous attention to detail I would construct the passenger basket of this gas balloon in my imagination and furnish it with every convenience. In its external appearance it resembled the basket I had once seen in a movie, but its equipment kept improving, until in the end it included all kinds of weird and wonderful electrical appliances and ingenious gadgets intended to come to my aid in an emergency...

In the taxi taking me from Lydda airport to Jerusalem I returned in my imagination to the heavy furniture and stuffy air in Aunt Flora's apartment. And when the taxi started climbing the hills at the approach to the city I saw the two huge photographs of her parents in my mind's eye. They were hanging on two pine trees on either side of the road leading up to Shoresh: on the right the picture of her buxom mother with her kindly eyes and flat nose, and on the left that of her father, a thin, bony man with a fez perched on the back of his head. For a moment the whole wadi was transformed into Aunt Flora's parlor, and the skeletons of the rusty armored cars at the sides of the road turned into a sideboard, a chair or a cupboard. The big clock with the pendulum too, which looked like a steel helmet, peeped at me though the pine trees.

It was eleven o'clock in the morning.

My father also had never mentioned my mother. When I was in the fourth or fifth grade I learned that my mother, who had disappeared from our lives some time before, was still alive, and that she was living in a place where my father visited her every month. These visits were shrouded in mystery. When I grew older I too was permitted to see her. Beside myself with excitement, in fear and trembling, I prepared myself for the first visit. Mother was young, beautiful and remote. She was only seventeen years older than me. And now, for the first time in my life, I resolved to visit her regularly and often, and as my eyes filled with tears she rose before me, strange and remote, inaccessible, imprisoned behind threatening walls which I was determined to breach, come what may.

When I reached home I threw my bags onto the bed and I was already on my way to her, when I heard a faint rustle at my side. It's my father come to guide me, I said to myself, and passages from his diary appeared unbidden before my eyes:

> 12 November 1949: I returned to the camp from home leave with the other members of our cell. Now we are soldiers in a regular army, we are the veterans, reservists, and the eighteen-year-old recruits look ridiculous to us. Some of them were in youth battalions in Jerusalem during the war. One of them, with burning eyes, can't stop talking about what he saw in Deir Yassin last year (yes, hard to believe, it was a year and a half ago). He was seventeen at the time. Rather modestly, he explains that he was second in command of a section. Over and over again, like a scratched record, he repeats: 'We came to clean up after you, we removed the bodies of the Arab villagers you massacred.' We pay no attention to his rantings....
>
> A strong smell of soap pervades the lorry climbing the hill. It will soon fade, and be replaced by the smell of sweat and cigarette smoke given off by us, the thirty soldiers packed into the back. Then the smell of the gun oil will cling to us and become part of us, as if someone has greased our wrists, our knees and our ankles and all the hinges of our bodies with this horrible oil....
>
> Soon we will become a consolidated military unit, no longer isolated underground cells as in the past. I'm forty-four years old, a boy in the forties of his life. What do I see when I look behind my shoulder? My

comrades in the struggle, my various missions, my love for Benhazar? Or perhaps my accomplishments as an amateur historian? Everything is swept up in one great storm.

Not one word about Mother! This thought would not go away. I stood leaning against the wall of the Belgian consulate in Salameh Square, waiting for my father to leave me so that I could go and visit my mother. But once more I was trapped in my reflections. In my father's diaries, on a ripped-out page rescued from the fire, I found the following passage:

> 30 November 1949: They've made me a section commander, on the grounds of my experience. What experience? Robbing a bank? Smashing a window and stealing a couple of typewriters for the organization? Beating up the boy from Haifa who "sang" to Sergeant Peter Morton and told him everything he wanted to hear?....
> Reserves, yes we're in the reserves. A ridiculous term. Where did they find it? Reserves of what? Reserves of strength? Reserves of will? Reserves of what? Some state we've established. A caricature of a state. My head rests against the tarpaulin of the army truck. I doze and daydream. Benhazar, you are all my hope. In front of me lies a vast flat plain, and nothing else.

I was moved. Only now did I realize the full meaning of these last words. My eyes filled with tears. A kind of last will and testament. I give up, I said to myself, and dredged up another page of what remained of my father's diary from my memory. There was no date on it. My father described at length how five youngsters from the Hebrew Gymnasium in Rechavia – four boys and one girl – were attached to his platoon, which was on its way to shooting practice near Rosh Pinna in the framework of reserve duty. He contemplated the five youngsters for a long time, and during a break in the training (or perhaps when the reserve duty was over) he wrote:

> You had no part in the struggle of the Hebrew people. Your songs are foreign and remote. You, Iris, sitting next to Nissim, your head resting lightly against his shoulder, swaying your body as if in time to some distant melody. A kerchief bound tightly round your head – in Ioannina we called it a *yazma*. My mother rebelled against it because it constricted her thoughts and denied her freedom, and now, here, in the free State of Israel, it's the latest fashion! A colored *yazma* and short pants. One girl in a truck full of men. Iris stole a glance at me, and then another one. How far have I fallen from the Promenade in Ioannina? What will become of me? Please, God.

OK, I give up. I won't go to Mother. I'll stay with you, Father. You're not alone.

I have never understood the nature of the relationship between my parents. One thing I knew: there was a very big gap in age between them. But was this the reason they lived apart for so many years? Was this why my mother was taken from me and shut up in an institution?

Sometimes I thought that she had no alternative but to retreat and withdraw little by little, at first into her own mind, and then behind the walls of an institution. This was the only way she could protect herself from her husband's enormous energy, from the mystery and the danger surrounding him. She knew that he was defying mysterious forces that he should never have taken on, for he had appointed himself to the post of leader and commander without permission from anybody and without a single soldier to carry out his orders.

When she was still a girl she gave birth to me, and she was immediately abandoned by my father. She was followed by the British secret police, who gave her no rest. She did not want to trouble relatives and friends. My father's comrades in the underground too harassed her. On more than one occasion she was on the point of starving and with me in her arms she wandered the silent streets of Jerusalem in search of food.

"She had a hard time," Kalamaro said to me once – and left it at that.

In the end she broke down.

I roused myself from my memories, and from Salameh Square I turned towards Lepers' Lane, but before I reached the hospital walls, I turned left in the direction of the Rose Garden.

"I'm going to my mother," I said aloud, and looked around me to see if anyone had noticed my sudden joy.

In my childhood I was afraid of walking down Lepers' Lane by myself, and whenever I was on the point of doing so, I would recoil at the last minute and go home disappointed but determined to pass the test next time.

The two walls that imprisoned the steep, narrow lane between them, threatening to close it in completely, excited the imaginations of my peers. On the left rose the wall of the lepers' hospital, and on the right the wall of the Bank House. Bits of broken colored glass were stuck on top of both walls, endangering anyone who dared climb them in order to peep into the world behind them.

The Bank House served as an exclusive club for the upper echelons of Barclays Bank, and was also the residence of Mr. Clark, the manager of the Jerusalem branch of the bank. A stern-faced guard was stationed at the gate, which was opposite the entrance to the lepers' hospital. As a child I didn't know what purpose the building served, and saw it, too, as belonging to the world of the lepers. At night, when the moon sailed between the pines and cypresses of the wood, I believed that the patients with their disfigured faces and mutilated bodies crossed the lane in their white gowns from the hospital to the opposite wall, and with unimaginable sorrow glittering in their eyes threatened the healthy inhabitants of the city, going complacently about their business with no idea of the danger threatening them.

Whenever I thought of them a cold shiver ran down my spine. And now too I walked slowly along the eastern wall, the hospital wall, trying to think of something to calm my nerves, and I remembered a story my uncle once told me about Mr. Clark's pampered pet pelican. This bird lived next to the ornamental pond in the bank manager's garden and every day it was fed with fresh fish brought from Jericho by Mr. Clark's driver. Every day the driver would drive down the winding road to Jericho in the grand Vauxhall, to the fishmonger Abu Salim, in order to satisfy the pelican's fastidious appetite and endear himself to his master, who delighted in watching his pet gobble up the fish.

Suddenly I looked over my shoulder, and an eerie sensation took hold of me. Were my eyes deceiving me? Had the wall of the Bank House really come tumbling down? I stood still and turned around, and overcome by astonishment I contemplated the marvel that had taken place here while I was away. The mysterious wall had disappeared and not a trace remained of the building behind it. And where was the pelican? Where did the lepers from the hospital go now on moonlit nights?

I continued on my way and walked past the Rose Garden, unable to tear my eyes away from the great metal lamp hanging over the southern gate of the park. Here, exactly here, I had been photographed with my mother and father in those distant days, happy days that would never return. Here I am standing in short pants with suspenders, with my old-fashioned haircut, with my little eyes: and here is my father in his striped suit with the wide lapels, with his hat in his hand. At his side stands my mother, smiling, content, her hair up in a bun and her shapely figure clad in a narrow-skirted suit of the kind that has disappeared off the face of the earth.

Thus I arrived at the blocked-off rear entrance of the hospital, and after a brief hesitation, I turned quickly onto Alkalai Street, and from there, walking faster and faster, almost running, right onto the bottom of Disraeli Street.

At the entrance to my mother's hospital, the Talbiyeh mental hospital, I saw Kalamaro's car, with its roof down. It was a small brown 1948 Morris Minor, unique in Jerusalem and perhaps in the entire country. Unlike a collector's car, it wasn't a cherished, gleaming museum piece. It showed the evidence of every passing year and every line on its owner's forehead. It was worn out with use.

Impatiently I knocked on the iron door set inside the wide hospital gates. This little door was for the use of pedestrians, while the big gate (was it ever opened?) was for the commercial vans bringing equipment and supplies to the hospital. A door within a door, like a heart within a heart – when the big one opened, the little one was cancelled out, but when the little one opened, the big one remained, concealing and threatening.

The guard opened up, and without saying a word, with a jerk of his head, invited me in. Anyone prepared to come here, he said once, is welcome. As soon as I stepped into the garden I noticed Kalamaro in his white suit and shoes. The hair on his head too, was shining white. A tall, thin man, standing and preaching a sermon to a group of patients clustered round him on a curve in the garden path. Every one of the people standing in that strange circle saw what he wanted to see in the proud old man – Messiah, father, leader, preacher or angel just descended from heaven. But I doubted if any of his audience understood the sermons I knew so well.

"Could anything like that have happened when the British were here?" he asked his audience excitedly. He was in the middle of a story about a repair needed for his car, angry at the fact that the spare part required was not available in any garage in Israel – "a country so successful in all the complicated technological fields connected to war." Then he turned to the question of the breaching of the "Green line" because of the "last round between us and the Arabs," which brought us closer, in his opinion, "to our brothers who still preserve a little of the spirit of the British Mandate," and he continued passionately: "Look at their officials, their policemen and their judges. Look at their polite, industrious shopkeepers. In addition to other virtues more precious than gold, they also have honor and integrity. Yes, my friends, honor and integrity." And therefore

Kalamaro now demanded the speedy return of the Land of Israel to the British, whose influence in the areas of economics and administration would oblige us to shake off the absurd nationalistic notions into which we had sunk. Only thus, he insisted, would peace and quiet come to the region. And in a practical tone he suggested applying to Harold Wilson and asking him to come back and resume the responsibility for governing Palestine.

It was evident that his audience were captivated by his charm and his arguments. Two of the more enthusiastic among them even began shouting rhythmically, looking at each other gleefully and exposing their rotten teeth as they opened their dribbling mouths wide: "Bring back the British! Bring back the British!"

But Kalamaro silenced his disciples and ordered them to disperse as he suddenly caught sight of me. An expression of mild embarrassment crossed his face, but he quickly recovered and hurried with broad strides towards me.

"Benazariko's arrived, Benazariko's arrived!" he cried joyfully and slapped me on the shoulder. When he looked back at his audience, who had remained where they were, two of them shouted after him, gazing up at the sky with their eyes shining: "Benazariko's arrived, Benazariko's arrived!"

So far from dispersing, the crowd seemed to have grown. From the paths and benches more and more patients came hurrying up, as if to witness the fulfillment of their Messiah's prophecy, the return of the High Commissioner to his seat of government here in Talbiyeh.

"Cunningham," someone suddenly whispered.

"Cunningham, Cunningham," the name reverberated from one end of the garden to the other.

"*Koenig, Koenig,*" explained one of the patients in Yiddish to the dark-skinned friend leaning on his shoulder. "Don't you understand? *Koenig.*"

"King, king," a third made haste to explain, and his whisper, which sounded alarmed at first, gathered confidence from one moment to the next.

I stood there appalled.

"Kalamaro, stop this dreadful nonsense at once," I demanded.

"My dear friends," Kalamaro roused himself, "please return to your rooms. It's time for dinner."

And the voices began to subside. They had apparently concluded that the promised redemption was not yet at hand, and each of them had better return to the thoughts of his own disturbed mind, or at least satisfy his hunger.

We were left alone, and Kalamaro embraced me warmly, rolling his eyes theatrically, and asked, "Where were you, Benazariko? Where did you disappear to?"

I shrank back slightly and didn't answer. I asked him, "Have you seen her?"

"Of course, my boy, of course," he said reproachfully. "I visit her often. Who has she got in the world apart from you and me? And since you've been wandering around the world lately I took it on myself to look after her. I'll take you to her at once. I haven't seen her yet today."

We began walking towards the main building. But on our way there Kalamaro, to my annoyance, stopped a couple times to answer the questions of a number of his fans, who accosted him with timid smiles and eyes full of bewilderment but also admiration. "Maybe we should bring the British back here ourselves?" suggested one of them – a middle aged man with grey stubble covering his cheeks and veiled green eyes. "One of my cousins is a pilot, so maybe he can collect the British in his plane and bring them here?" And his friend who had a bad limp and a broad, red runny nose argued that we should open the gates of the Land of Israel to illegal immigration of Englishmen, and he even instructed Kalamaro to acquire a few old freight ships which could be bought cheaply and filled with as many British solders as possible with their weapons and equipment, and smuggled in at night past the patrol ships of the Israeli navy, and even if some of them were caught a lot of the others would reach the shore. And here they would be organized in underground cells and when the signal was given (by Kalamaro, of course) they would seize power and bring peace and prosperity to Israel.

I tugged impatiently at Kalamaro's sleeve, and urged him repeatedly, "Come on, already, take me to my mother." But even before we reached the building we saw her, sitting on her knees in the shade of a tree, in a broad basin which had just been watered, a blissful, dreamy expression on her face. She was wearing a white dress and sandals with a white hat trimmed with a white scarf on her head. Her face was brown and beautiful. She looked to me like an angel.

I went up to her and stood stock still. Her lashes were long, her eyes blue, her lips full and her bosom broad. At first she didn't notice me; she was absorbed in a silent prayer, and her face, like her kneeling body, was full of devotion and wonder.

"Mother," I cried in a whisper, "my mother."

A force stronger than I was felled me to the ground. I knelt down beside her and sank into the soft mud. My arms encircled her head. Again and again I kissed her cheeks and the heavy weight that had been lying on my heart like a stone for many months dissolved into a stream of tears. And she turned her head in surprise towards Kalamaro, who was standing over us on the edge of the muddy basin, as if to ask him the meaning of this unexpected interruption. Then, like a small child extricating itself from the embrace of an unfamiliar relative, she stood up, a dripping brown stain on the back of her dress, her hands full of mud, and turned away. But suddenly she stopped, turned around and looked at me, and her hands began mechanically stroking my cheeks, leaving moist brown streaks which made me look like an American Indian warrior. I stood up and took her hand, and we left the little grove of trees with our arms around each other and Kalamaro behind us.

"You know, Daddy was here today," she said in a cheerful voice. "He gave me his weekly note and asked me to pass it on to you. It's a very important note."

"Yes, Mother. I'd like to see Daddy too."

"Next time he comes the three of us will be together."

We walked up the path leading to the building where she lived. Like a country woman she took off her soaked sandals, fastened the straps together and hung them over her shoulder – two birds trapped in the woods – one dangling down her back and the other on her chest.

"Let's go inside," we heard Kalamaro's voice behind us, in a hurry to get away from his admirers.

Mother received special treatment in the hospital – she was the only patient who had a little room to herself. On the door I saw a ceramic sign, a little Armenian tile decorated with colorful flowers, upon which an unpracticed hand had written: "Irena Cohen, welcome all." That must be a present from Kalamaro, I said to myself. Now the old man stepped quickly in front of us, opened the door, ushered us in, and made haste to shut it again.

The room was spotlessly clean, and despite the crude mustard-colored oil paint going halfway up the walls, the atmosphere was comfortable and even cozy. The iron bed was neatly made. Next to it stood a little brown chest of drawers, and on it a vase of green Hebron glass containing daisies standing as stiffly as soldiers, which had apparently been picked in the field next to the Rose Garden, not far from the Nature Museum.

Mother took off her hat and threw it onto the bed. Her muddy sandals she placed carefully on a sheet of newspaper, next to the little wash basin in the corner of the room. After that she washed her hands and face, deftly crossed her arms, gripped her dress, pulled it over her head and remained standing in the middle of the room, naked as the day she was born. Then she walked over to the ancient closet, cracked but gleaming, next to the door, quickly took out a white dress, exactly like the one she had just taken off, and with one practiced movement pulled it onto her youthful, shapely body. After that she lay down on the bed with her legs tucked under her. Without hesitation, as if he was used to it, Kalamaro picked up the soiled dress she had left lying in the middle of the room, and put it in the wicker basket under the basin. And I, after standing stunned and silent all this time, looked out the barred window to make sure that all this was really happening, that it wasn't a dream, and I saw the tangled barbed wire fence stretched sloppily on top of the hospital wall, and the ugly inner courtyard strewn with tins and rusty buckets.

Kalamaro sat down on an old armchair. Nobody said a word. I picked up the transistor radio I found on the window sill and examined it thoroughly from all sides, as if I had never seen anything like it before, glanced at my watch and turned the top button with an absentminded air. The last notes of a Bach fugue rose into the air, and then the signature tune announcing the news. It was five o'clock. The newscaster reported the events of the day in the war of attrition being waged in the region of the Suez Canal and the Jordan Valley. In the Jordan Valley another terrorist attempt to penetrate an IDF post had been repulsed, and the far-flung search for the perpetrators that had begun at dawn had not yet produced any results.

"It's a bad situation. We haven't got a hope of getting ourselves out of the mess we've landed ourselves in," sighed Kalamaro. "The coming elections won't bring any change either."

"Yes," I said.

"In the Great War," Kalamaro began to bask in his memories of the First World War, "I was among those who crossed the Jordan River and liberated the country from the yoke of the Turks. Joshua the son of Nun also conquered the land from the East. Anyone who thinks we can take this country for granted is doomed. Why on earth did we send the British packing?"

"Jochanan also thought that the Japanese and their Indian friends should come from the East to help us," said my mother with a glazed look in her eyes, shifting restlessly on her bed. "You, Kalamaro, brought the British here; Jochanan wanted to get rid of them."

I tensed. This was the first time I had ever heard my mother talk about the subject to which I had recently devoted so much time and thought. Up to now I had dismissed the possibility of getting anything about my father's affairs out of her. I signaled Kalamaro to keep quiet and said quickly, "You're right, Mother. Tell us more about what Daddy thought."

My mother sighed, dropped her bare feet over the edge of the bed, slipped under it like an agile cat, and immediately emerged again with a brown cardboard box crammed with papers.

"This was exactly what Jochanan's correspondence with Fujiwara, in charge of setting up the Indian National Army on behalf of the Tokyo Imperial Command, was about. They wrote to each other often. It's all written here." And she tapped the sides of the box.

My eyes almost popped out of their sockets. Suddenly the obscure accusation hurled at me by the fireman in my father's burnt room in Rutenberg Lane echoed in my ears. "You and that crazy woman in white! All you care about is your papers! She snatched the papers from the flames and went up in smoke herself!" I had traveled all the way to Great Britain and distant Hong Kong to discover his lost tracks, while all the time such important material was right here, in Talbiyeh, with my mother, and I knew nothing about it.

"And what did Daddy want?" I asked quickly, before her mind strayed to another subject.

Kalamaro began to say something, but he was silenced by the warning expression on my face. My mother went on holding the cardboard box, shielding it with her arms like a mother warding off danger to her child, and she didn't answer me. Once more she disappeared behind a blank wall.

Dr. Emile Schechter, the head of the department, a short, plump, balding man, came into the room without knocking. When he saw me and Kalamaro he smiled, looked a little embarrassed and went up to my mother's bed.

"And how are we today, Mrs. Cohen?" he asked in a loud, clear voice.

She didn't reply.

I went up to the doctor, held out my hand and introduced myself.

"Your mother has mentioned you a number of times during the past year," said Dr. Schechter.

"Actually, I've been abroad," I said quickly, as if to justify my lengthy absence. I knew that I was misleading the doctor, since I hadn't come to visit her before leaving the country either. "Before my father used to visit her," I added for some reason.

"We were very fond of Mr. Cohen," said Dr. Schechter. "We were sorry to hear about his tragic death. You know, young Mr. Cohen, that your mother disappeared on the night your father died? She vanished into thin air, as if the earth had swallowed her up."

"No, I didn't know."

"The next day at dawn we found her here in her room, sitting on this armchair," he said and pointed to the chair on which Kalamaro was now sitting, "as if nothing had happened. Only this box had been added to her possessions. Don't ask me what it means. I have no explanation," he sighed as if admitting failure.

"How is she?" I asked.

"There's no change. She has to keep taking her medication, following her daily routine. It's the only way." He was on the point of turning round and leaving the room.

"Perhaps it would be possible to make her more communicative," I said. "Perhaps it would be possible to reduce her medication and to try other methods of therapy? I suppose there must be new developments in the field?"

Even in my own ears my words sounded unconvincing, and I therefore quickly added, "Perhaps now that I'm here, it would be possible to take her for a little walk outside the hospital? Perhaps a miracle would happen?"

"You young people know everything," said the doctor sternly and waved his hand in irritable dismissal. "They know everything," he repeated, this time to Kalamaro, who kept getting up and sitting down again, and was now standing tall and impressive next to the little doctor.

"It was just a thought," I retreated.

"You know, young Mr. Cohen, that your mother has been here for sixteen years. This is her home. Here she lives her life. Don't try to be cleverer than everybody else. We have all the necessary experience." He hesitated for a moment, as if trying to make up his mind about something, and the expression on his face changed. In a more relaxed tone he added, "As for a little walk, perhaps we could consider it. But you should know that the moment your mother leaves the hospital we cease to be responsible for her, and the entire expedition will be the family's responsibility."

And he took his leave and walked out of the room.

"And now you can go, Benhazar. You only came back today. Go and lie down, have a rest and come again next week," said Kalamaro.

I was, indeed, tired, and my thoughts were whirling around in my mind. I needed rest, a decent sleep, and time, in order to consider the situation with a clear head. My mother was sunk deep in her private world, and I kissed her on the forehead, nodded to Kalamaro and left.

Chapter Seven

I sat in my room. On the table in front of me lay a photocopy of an article by the American scholar Joyce Lebra on the armies trained by the Japanese during the Second World War. Suharto, Ne Win and Park, she argued, were not just the leaders of military bureaucracies in Indonesia, Burma and Korea, they were also united by the historical fact that they were all educated in army units and military schools under Japanese control. The Indian National Army, the Burma Independence Army and the Army of Defenders of the Homeland in Indonesia – the "PETA" – were the creations of the Japanese occupying regime in Southeast Asia. In other places too, Japan had a decisive military and political influence on the historical process that led to political independence in Asia and liberation from the yoke of Western imperialism.

I raised my eyes from the printed pages and looked through the open window at the flourishing pine tree whose roots were fixed deep in the yard of my neighbor Professor Tur-Sinai and whose branches brushed my windowsill. It was one o'clock in the afternoon. Everything was still. The chirping of birds and the distant hooting of the train going down to the coastal plain emphasized the silence. I was pleased, greatly encouraged by the article I had just read, which even though it did not deal with Palestine, enabled me to conclude that my father's policy of rapprochement to Japan had not been lacking in sense, or even in perspicacity. If he had been wrong, it was only in his tactical considerations.

The criticism levelled at him, whether at the time or later, had always weighed heavily on me, as his son. Now, for the first time, I was convinced by the credo of the political realist: to act responsibly, but within the limits of the information available at the time. More than that was impossible to demand. My father should not be judged ahistorically, with the benefit of hindsight. It was unfair to see his actions in the light of their consequences (or the lack of them). For the consequences of a course of action depend on many diverse variables, some of which are impossible to predict. Sometimes intelligent, rational, and pertinent decisions lead to bad and disappointing results, and sometimes vice versa. The more I immersed myself in studying the period and the nature of the dilemmas facing my father and his friends, the more I understood what my father had done. At the same time I tried to convince myself that I was being rational and objective and that my opinions were not influenced by my family connection.

When, in the months following the murder of Yair, the head of the "Stern Gang," the rumors of the dimensions of the systematic extermination of European Jewry were verified, the members of the underground changed their minds and cancelled their plans to collaborate with the foe. But not only my father and his friends had been mistaken in their evaluation of the situation; people regarded as responsible and sound, people who held central positions in the leadership of the Jewish population of Palestine, made grave mistakes during the period in question. Their mistakes had not yet been fully exposed, but all kinds of journalists and historians had already started hinting at them, in speech and in writing. I remembered the 1956 Kastner affair in which it had been argued that the Jewish Agency had miscalculated regarding the possibility of saving Hungarian Jews with all its political implications. But, intent on my mission, I banished it from my mind at once: even established politicians can fall victim to unexpected circumstances, make "optical" errors, and they too deserve understanding and forgiveness. If only they had stopped persecuting people who didn't think like them, who refused to accept their authority, their forgiveness might be absolute. But they went on harassing their political opponents, and my father, as one of them, knew no peace until the day he died. For apart from the condemnation and humiliation to which they were subjected at the time of their underground activities, accusations of shortsightedness and political lunacy pursued them for years afterwards.

And my father suffered even more than the others, for nobody, not even his closest friends and comrades, was prepared to embrace his Asian passion or accept his view that from the end of 1942 Japan was destined to undertake the historic role previously played by its allies in Europe. My father could not understand why his friends were unable to go along with him even after the war broke out in the Far East, and why Spielberg, R. Avior, Solomonovitz and many others refused to take his ideas seriously, and consider them within the framework of the national anti-imperialist debate. After all, the Japanese, for all their undeniable cruelty, as in the rape of Nanking, could not be accused of racism or systematic extermination. ("If a new orientation was required, could it ignore the Orient?" I found in one of my father's jottings.) And therefore the Jews in Palestine, here, in Western Asia, had to recognize the historic importance of Japan, which had acted to rid the continent of European imperialism and to establish an autonomous Asian order. And if they failed to do so, the failure was due to mistaken calculations and to an exaggerated Eurocentric approach that showed a lack of openness and an inability to come to bold and original conclusions.

But it wasn't only that my father's friends disagreed with his views. There was a kind of collectivism of thought and deed in the underground, and anyone who deviated from it found himself isolated and even in danger of losing his life. Here I remembered the "Bashani affair," which my father had hinted at on a couple of occasions: the body of Eliezar Bashani was found one morning on the Tel Aviv beach, not far from the promenade. The British CID insisted that he had been murdered as a result of an internal underground conflict. The British had been looking for Bashani, but this was not the way they wanted to find him. The authorities waited a few days for someone, family or friend, to approach them and ask for the body, but nobody turned up. When he was finally buried in the Tel Aviv cemetery, with the help of a rabbi, detectives were sent to spy on the mourners, but they failed to come up with a suspect. Was my father haunted by the "Bashani affair"? Was he afraid that he too would pay for his independent opinions and initiatives with his life?

I went on reading eagerly, unable to stop even when the letters danced before my tired eyes. "In Asia," wrote Joyce Lebra, "the armies trained by the Japanese were the agents of modernization and progress...."

The telephone rang and returned me to the present. It was Yonit Harmelech, a friend from my army days, now studying biology at Hebrew University. She was a brisk, calculating young woman who pursued her academic career with a zeal that left nothing to chance. She was now on the point of completing her second degree and embarking confidently on the third, the longed-for PH.D. Our meetings were accidental and casual. I avoided getting any closer to her and since my return to the country a few weeks before I had only met her once, next to the Comfort shoe shop on Ben Yehuda Street. For some reason, this meeting reminded me of a few lines written by my father:

...I met her, after a long time had passed, at the top of Ben Yehuda Street, and her eyes no longer spoke to me. She asked me again where I was living. I must be careful! I nodded to her and hurried away.

Now, in a strange coincidence, I heard Yonit asking me over the phone whether I was going to stay in my parents' apartment. I didn't answer. In my Jerusalem the neighborhood where a person lives has a profound significance, I thought. The neighborhood is a part of the person. It's much more important than "quality of life," that empty concept which became current together with the great deterioration of life in Jerusalem. I had no desire to talk to her or anyone else, and I kept quiet, mulling over the thought that a true Jerusalemite can't make a "rational" choice of where to live, like the invaders from the coastal plain who began settling in Jerusalem after the unification of the city. A Jerusalemite is part of his neighborhood, or he isn't a Jerusalemite at all.

"Hello, Benhazar, can you hear me?" called Yonit.

"I read you clearly. Repeat: clearly. Over," I tried to make a joke of it by recalling the days when our company was deployed on the Syrian border on the eve of the raid on Nukaib.

She giggled and waited.

"I'm terribly busy," I heard myself saying, "you know, problems with my mother, tons of arrangements to make – I'll get in touch with you later in the week."

"'Bye for now," she said and hung up.

On a piece of paper lying on the table, on which I had scribbled broken lines, snails, and little breasts while reading the article and talking to Yonit, I jotted down my father's movements during World War II.

At my meeting with Woodhead I had learned that my father had reached Hong Kong about two weeks before the attack on Pearl Harbor and the conquest of the colony by the Japanese. During this period, at the end of November 1942, he had posed as a student of Japanese history. Under the watchful eyes of British intelligence he made contact with low-level Japanese agents (a few of them double agents), who were preparing the ground for tightening the bonds between Tokyo and the national leaders of Southeast Asia before mounting the attack on white imperialism. The British intended to set a trap for my father, but they gave in to the temptation to wait until they could gather as much evidence as possible against him and find out exactly who his operators were, and thus paved the way for their embarrassing failure: not only did they fail to find any connection between him and his "operators" in Palestine, they lost track of him completely in a short space of time.

The person they called "J.C." vanished from the colony, and all their attempts to find him failed. The dire, fateful days that descended on the area, and in fact on the whole world, distracted the British from local problems to the great problem of survival in their strongholds, and afterwards to the question of returning to the colonies from which they had been expelled by the Japanese.

My father's movements until the end of 1942 were not clear to me. I was unable to extract any significant information from the veterans of the underground in Israel. I had managed to track down Spielberg, who knew a lot and was even in possession of a great deal of archive material, but he refused to talk to me, even on the phone. Nor was I able to discover what their attitude towards my father was. One thing was clear: their attitude to me, his inquisitive son, was one of avoidance, and even hostility. Accordingly, what I nevertheless did manage to discover I had to deduce and patch together by my own unaided efforts – in spite of the people he regarded as his friends. I was able to determine only one fact for certain: my father returned to Palestine at the end of 1942 and remained there for the whole of 1943. And then, especially after a number of the members of the group escaped from British detention, he was active in the underground. During those days I was born. In a photograph in my possession my father is holding me in his arms, apparently in the Rose Garden. On the back of the photograph are the words "Benhazar at three months. December 1943."

In the spring of 1944 Woodhead and the rest of the British intelligence in New Delhi received information about a white man in Subhas Chandra Bose's camp in Burma. Three months later his identity was established – Jochanan Cohen. What was my father doing there? I was unable to come up with a complete answer to this question, but I knew that during the period in question the Japanese were busy planning their attack on British India in the Imphal and Kohima regions, while at the same time the British were preparing to retake Burma. They hoped to seize the north of the country and thus to open the road for the allied forces, the Chinese and the Americans, to enter China. This complicated campaign was to be commanded by General Slim.

Facing the British forces was the Japanese General Kawabe, commander of all the Japanese forces in Burma. One of the armies under his command was charged with isolating Imphal, where the British were in control, and taking the area next to the airfields, with their food stores and equipment. Another force was charged with taking Kohima and holding it. From this strategic point the Japanese hoped to penetrate the Assam valley and deny the British access to the airfields from which supplies and ammunition were flown to the fighting Chinese, and also to bar the way to the Chinese and American forces that were about to break through the Japanese lines and enter China. At this point the Japanese intended sending the pro-Japanese Indian National Army – Bose's men – into India in the hope of provoking a general uprising against the British, and perhaps paving the way to influencing events in the Persian Gulf and West Asia.

However, although at first the Japanese seemed close to succeeding in their plans, on the twenty-second of June the British mounted a counterattack from Dimapur, joined up with another force a few kilometers north of Imphal, and repulsed the enemy. The threat to British India was removed.

Only at the end of 1944, or perhaps at the beginning of 1945, did my father end his mysterious journey and return to Palestine. Here he took part in anti-British activities again, but of this I knew next to nothing. For example, I didn't know if it was the harsh British reaction to the attack mounted by the Irgun and Lechi on the central British prison in Jerusalem that led to his flight from the country. But one thing was clear to me, just as it was clear to my Aunt Sarina: it was the ground burning under his feet that sent him back to the land of his birth, to Greece, where he spent some time in Ioannina, with those members of his family who had survived the war.

My father's connection with the Japanese and their Indian supporters continued to preoccupy me. I read everything I could lay my hands on about Japanese policy and operations in the Asian arena from the beginning of the thirties to the end of the war, but the question of "planning versus muddling through" remained a riddle to me. Greater experts than myself were unable to determine with any degree of certainty whether Japan had intended in advance to conquer Asia, or if the civilian authorities, including the Emperor, had been dragged by the army into pursuing a policy they were not at all interested in. One thing was clear: at the end of the thirties government agencies in Tokyo were busy making a thorough study of national movements in Southeast Asia. And they weren't doing it out of academic interest, but as part of a long-term plan.

Young officers (under the aegis of the "Second Office" of the Imperial General Staff) were sent to the region, where they gathered and passed on information about the political, social and economic conditions. India, although it was not initially part of the area in which the Japanese were interested, gradually became an important factor in the plans for the defense of the Western flank of the projected Japanese area of influence. From India military and civilian supplies were sent to China, India's old enemy, and it also played an important role in the propaganda war in Asia, with the exploitation of the growing tension between the Indian national movement and British imperialism. Crushing the British forces and smashing the myth of the invincible Empire therefore became a vital condition for the success of the "New Order" in Asia – an order under the patronage of the Japanese. This, at any rate, was the view taken by the activist elements in Japan.

Subhas Chandra Bose, the great Indian leader from the radical bloc in Bengal, first took up residence in Berlin and tried to gain the support of the Germans for his cause, but at the end of 1941 and the beginning of 1942 he began to despair of receiving concrete help for the Indian independence movement from that quarter, and started putting out feelers towards Japan, which increasingly appeared to him as the faithful representative and enthusiastic supporter of Asian aspirations to liberate themselves from the yoke of European imperialism.

The figure of Subhas Chandra Bose inflamed my imagination. Did my father, too, share his political extremism, his fanaticism which bordered on madness? My thoughts carried me far away, to alien landscapes, unknown problems, unfamiliar experiences, and for a moment I saw myself as him, and I felt that the posture of my body in the chair, the expression on my face and even the way I held the pen in my hand were decisive proof that my father had not departed this world, that he was here, albeit in a different guise, but here.

Immediately my mother's face appeared among the pine needles opposite my window, my mother who I had visited frequently of late, trying to get her to talk to me, to mention the name of Fujiwara again, and perhaps even to let me see the letters that this Japanese officer had written to my father. But my mother would not permit anyone to touch the cardboard box in which, according to her, this correspondence was hidden.

On one of my visits I saw that the box had disappeared. When I asked her what had happened to it, she looked at me through a thick fog and smiled.

"Mother, please tell me about the connections between Daddy and Fujiwara," I begged.

"He was three years younger than your father," she suddenly volunteered. "Daddy met him in Bangkok, on the way to Hong Kong."

"Yes, go on," I urged her.

"Fujiwara had two good friends: Singh and Singh," she whispered and fell silent. Then she mumbled something, said "Singh and Singh" again, and that was it.

That day I left her angry and disappointed. But now, looking out of the open window, everything became clear and I could hardly contain my joy. I flipped rapidly through my notes. On his way to Hong Kong (in October or November of 1941), in neutral Thailand, my father met Fujiwara, who was studying the national question in India and Southeast Asia and maintained close connections with the leaders of the national movements there, in the hope that when the day came they would help him carry out the plans of the Imperial General Staff. Two Singhs played a prominent part in his plans: Pritam Singh, a religious leader and teacher, who led the Indian Independence League in Malaya and Thailand, and Mohan Singh. Relations of mutual trust and bonds of personal friendship grew up between Fujiwara and Mohan Singh.

Many months later, when the war was already raging, the Japanese reaped what they had sown before the war. Mohan Singh was one of the first Indian officers to be taken prisoner by the Japanese in central Malaya. The Japanese treated him not as a prisoner of war but as a friend. In the long discussions Fujiwara held with him, dwelling on the strong cultural, religious and historical bonds between India and Japan, he succeeded in igniting Singh's imagination and convincing him that the hour of India's liberation was at hand and that it would be achieved only by the desertion of as many Indian soldiers as possible from the British Indian army in Southeast Asia to the new army, the "Indian National Army," which would fight for the Indian nation and not for the defense of the British Empire. Thus Singh became one of the chief rebels against the British, a leader and prophet of the "New Order," who dedicated himself to the organization of the Indian National Army, which even before Singapore fell to the Japanese included about two thousand five hundred men.

Singapore fell three days after Yair was murdered in Tel Aviv. Forty-five thousand Indian soldiers were taken prisoner by the Japanese – a huge potential for the pro-Japanese Indian National Army. About half of the prisoners joined the new army after a mass rally in Farrer Park in Singapore during which Fujiwara and Mohan Singh made speeches explaining their plans.

Others joined the revolutionary army later, in the spring of 1943, when Subhas Chandra Bose arrived in the area and gave his support to the plan, thereby uniting the various strands of the anti-British protest movement into a single military force.

When I read about the rally in Farrer Park I felt sure that my father had been present on this historic occasion. But I didn't know if he already knew then that Yair had been murdered. If he did know, I said to myself, it must have strengthened his belief in the Asian plan; he must have seen the fall of Singapore as a swift and just punishment for the contemptible murder, and been sure that the time had come to act quickly and aggressively against the oppressive British regime in Palestine. There is no doubt that the connection with Japan appeared to him then as the only feasible way to deliver a death blow to the Empire, whose situation was almost desperate – if only everyone united against it, he must have said to himself, redemption would come more swiftly to the people of Israel in its land and the lives of many good men would be saved. And as time passed and rumors of the destruction of European Jewry multiplied, my father was no doubt strengthened in his belief that time was running out and the connection with Japan was the only solution.

Chapter Eight

The days went by and in my heart there was nothing but silence and emptiness. My visits to my mother became part of my weekly routine. After she had been institutionalized for so many years I saw no hope of any sudden improvement in her condition. I even put off my decision to take her out of the hospital, if only for a few hours, from one month to the next, perhaps because I was afraid of the experience, and perhaps because of Dr. Schechter's warning that any change in her routine could have adverse effects, for which I would be responsible.

But when I roamed the streets of the city on a Saturday morning, when the spring sunshine of Jerusalem drew me irresistibly out of the house, I couldn't avoid thinking of the possibility of "going for a walk with Mother" – which was how I put it to myself. And I thought of her more and more nowadays. Even though I knew that Kalamaro continued to visit her devotedly, taking care of all her needs and providing her with company and support, I felt profound concern together with my growing closeness to her, and a wish to do something to help her. And as if this wasn't enough, I kept on bumping into women I called "friends of the family" in the little neighborhood supermarket, and they, after questioning me briefly about the welfare of friends and relatives, would shake their heads and repeat reproachfully, "Dear Kalamaro, he's an angel, a real angel from heaven," and my heart would contract and I would immediately promise myself to do everything in my power to help my mother and make her lot easier to bear.

I began meeting Yonit more frequently. I was flattered by her attention, but her attitude to life, her calculating nature and her lack of spontaneity still put me off. On the other hand, I had to admit, I enjoyed putting a spoke in her wheels, proving to her that the only thing you could expect was the unexpected, and contradicting her on every possible point. For some reason I felt I had to prove to myself that I was stronger than she was, that even though she studied hard and planned every stage of her life in detail, I was better and quicker than she was. I often picked quarrels with her on trivial issues, even when I knew that she was right. She became a target for my barbs, playing a special role in my life at the time. While she advanced steadily along the route she had laid out for herself, I jumped about from one thing to another, justifying my behavior on the grounds of a complicated ideology that we both knew was baseless. In my heart of hearts I knew that my unending restlessness and my inability to stick to anything were the result of a profound inner turmoil, and I waited impatiently for the moment when the storm would subside and let me be, but at the same time I feared it.

I was staying in my parents' house, and living less on my modest and erratic earnings than on the assets of the family and the two hundred dollars that Sarina had been sending me every month since my visit to Hong Kong. To the check coming from the other end of the world she would attach a brief handwritten note which always ended with the same words: "*Kerido, keremos venir a Israel a il anyo venidero, besos, Sarina* (Dear, we want to come to Israel next year, kisses, Sarina)." For some reason she thought I was studying at the university, and she would always ask how I was getting on with my studies and when I would complete them. I saw no reason to correct this mistake, which gave me a pang whenever I received her checks and the letters that accompanied them.

One day, late in the afternoon, when I left the house I saw a group of boys dragging a number of dilapidated boxes full of planks, branches and twigs. "Lag Ba'omer 1971, the thirty-third day of the counting of the Omer, the 5731st year since the creation of the world," I said to myself, mocking my obsession with dates. And as usual, once I had begun calculating dates and periods I was in no hurry to change the subject: I worked out exactly how old I was, years, months and days – and dredged up from the depths of my memory the Lag Ba'omer bonfires of last year, the year before last, and the many bonfires that had preceded them; exactly where I had been, what I had done, what I had thought, how many times I had been with my friends, how many with my father, and mainly, how many times my mother had been with me.

For some reason this question seemed imbued with profound significance, I didn't know why. And then the memory of a distant bonfire somewhere at the edge of the Valley of the Cross gradually rose to the surface and all my thoughts focused on a single image: my mother and father standing facing the fire and smiling at me while I, full of excitement, approach the flames with a bundle of twigs in my hand, approach it bravely and resolutely, and then shrink back from the heat and retreat. Was this in 1949 or perhaps in 1950? Suddenly it seemed vitally important to know the exact year.

Back in Salameh Square I suddenly decided: this Lag Ba'omer I was going to celebrate with my mother. I would light a bonfire like we did twenty years ago, roast potatoes and a few onions, and we would sit and chat like in the old days.

I immediately cancelled the few vague plans I had for the evening, and went home full of satisfaction at the thought that I had not yet lost my spontaneity, that I could still act on the spur of the moment. Standing in the hall, in front of the round mirror which could have used a good polishing, I picked up the phone and called Yonit.

"Tonight," I announced with a cheerfulness that I rarely felt those days, "we're lighting a bonfire. Come over at seven."

"Great idea," enthused Yonit after a moment's hesitation, and immediately began to list everything we would require: eating utensils, paper napkins, salt and pepper, something to drink, toothpicks…

I didn't listen to what she was saying, thinking with satisfaction of the plans she had doubtlessly made for this evening and which she would now have to cancel. When she paused for a moment I said quickly, "Goodbye, see you later," and put the phone down.

Then I called the hospital and asked to speak to Dr. Schechter. I told him who I was and without any preamble asked if I could take my mother out for a walk this evening.

"Yes, yes, I take full responsibility," I heard myself saying, and listened to his instructions. When he was finished I took a deep breath.

Happy and excited I rushed around the apartment. In the kitchen I pulled a big plastic basket from the corner next to the fridge and filled it with potatoes, onions, a bag of coffee, a bag of sugar, and half a loaf of bread that was standing on the table. I took the basket with me to my room, where I took off my shoes, got undressed, removed a white shirt and white trousers from the closet and put them on in honor of the occasion. From the shoe drawer I took out a new pair of sneakers, also white, and put them on. Then I glanced at my watch and rushed into the stairwell. In the garden in front of the building I met Yonit, who was a few minutes early as usual. She looked prettier than usual in a white dress, her hair gathered in a bun, and her brown eyes smiling with anticipation.

"We're really crazy – wearing white to a bonfire. We'll come home black as chimneysweeps."

A pleasant surprise, I said to myself, at last no cold, logical, killjoy calculations. As if she had been infected by my own unusual mood. And then I noticed a big straw basket under her arm.

"I have everything here," she said, sounding both apologetic and pleased with herself.

"We're late," I said.

"Where are we going, Benhazar?"

"To my mother, of course," I answered in surprise. "My mother's waiting."

Yonit was astonished. Anxiety and disappointment darkened her face. She had never met my mother but she knew that she was very ill and had been hospitalized for years. She had never asked about her illness. And suddenly she knew. Actually she had known all along, but it was only now that she admitted what she knew. And immediately, so it seemed to me, the question she had avoided asking all this time posed itself: Had Benhazar inherited any of his mother's characteristics? Or perhaps it was the mere thought of visiting the "institution" that sent cold shivers down her spine.

"I don't take just anyone to see my mother," I tossed out and strode off. She took a few hesitant steps and the distance between us grew, and I turned my head and with a broad, almost military gesture indicated that she should hurry up.

"Wonderful," I suddenly heard her voice behind me, "let's go." She said this almost naturally, as if she had been waiting for months for just this opportunity, and with her head held high and a resolute expression on her face, she began running to catch up with me.

Puffing and panting after a rather long run we stood opposite the iron gates of the hospital. The pounding of Yonit's heart was evident in her face – from running? From fear? Her eyes followed every movement I made; she was obviously making a big effort to do the right thing and appear calm and natural.

I pounded on the gate with my fist. The gatekeeper opened up, and when we walked past him he called out, as if he had just remembered, "You just missed Kalamaro, he left a couple of minutes ago."

I said nothing and raced down the path leading to the building. Yonit was right behind me, but somehow she lost sight of me inside the building.

A few days later she told me how terrified she was when she entered the building and looked right and left in the big dark hallway without seeing me or hearing the echo of my footsteps. Two patients conferred in whispers in a distant corner to her right and a man in open pyjama pants advanced on her from the left. In growing panic she called out my name but I didn't answer. Instead broken figures of men appeared, peeping out of their dark rooms. She turned on her heel, about to return to the gatekeeper's hut, but on second thought she decided to stand her ground and deal with the foolish situation in which she found herself.

The man with the open fly was already standing near her, and with a toothless, dribbling mouth he inquired, as if in a series of hiccups, "May I be of assistance, madam?" Determined to remain calm and appear natural, she asked if he could direct her to Irena Cohen's room.

"You need the women's ward," the man replied with an affability that surprised her, "you have to go outside and go around the left side of the building."

She thanked him briefly and when she turned to go he fixed her with his eyes and asked, "Do you have a cigarette, madam?" And then his face suddenly contorted and Yonit froze in panic. It seemed to her that the man was about to thrust his face into hers, and trying to keep cool she began to rummage in her basket before murmuring, "No, I'm sorry, I don't smoke." But the rattling of the matches in the box she had brought with her to light the bonfire betrayed her.

"But you've got matches," the man sniggered.

Yonit's hand encountered a big apple in the basket and she quickly whipped it out and presented it to her interlocutor in the hope of distancing his face from hers. "Won't you have an apple?" she asked. "It's good for you," and at that moment she heard my voice. My mother was already with me. When I asked Yonit where she had disappeared to, she said that she had decided to wait for me here, gave the apple to the man in the pyjama pants, and started walking down the hallway. Altogether, her behavior on her first visit to the hospital impressed me, and her frank description of her feelings there made me feel closer to her.

I introduced her to my mother, who shook her hand limply and said nothing. Then she turned abruptly to the door, and we followed her outside. I saw Yonit looking admiringly at her fine figure, her brown skin as smooth as a girl's and her beautiful blue eyes. Now too my mother was wearing her white dress and her broad-brimmed straw hat trimmed with a white ribbon.

We left the grounds through the iron gate, and as we passed the gatekeeper I winked at him behind the backs of Mother and Yonit, and handed him the permit I had received from Dr. Schechter.

We walked up Disraeli Street. Neither my mother nor Yonit uttered a word, but I, in an elated mood, sang the praises of the weather. "Fantastic, simply fantastic, the air's so fresh and crisp."

My mother did not respond and Yonit nodded her head and didn't even complain about the smoke from the bonfires.

At Marcus Street we stopped.

"Come on, let's go to the wood," I said.

We turned left at the descent into Lepers' Lane. On our left rose the wall of the lepers' hospital, and to our right stretched the little wood, with the wall that had until recently protected it leveled to the ground. Among the trees scattered bonfires appeared and children's loud, merry voices rose into the air.

"Isn't it delightful," I said, and Yonit nodded again.

Mother remained silent.

Next to the gate of the lepers' hospital we turned sharply into the wood, close to the place where the wall of the Bank House had stood a few years before. There we climbed a little mound of earth and started walking between the rocks of the wood.

"Here," I pointed to my right and said, "there once lived a beautiful, pampered pelican, and there," I pointed to the left, "stood the house of the British bank manager, Mr. Clark."

"Yes, I remember," my mother's voice surprised me.

We tensed, but she fell silent without saying any more.

"Danger!" we suddenly heard a frightened child's voice.

A commotion broke out around us. Right next to us we heard an infant crying. In an instant children came hurrying up from all sides, abandoning their affairs – feeding their fires, roasting their food and collecting firewood – when they saw that it was not a false alarm, that three strange figures in white had invaded the woods and were gliding about among the trees. For a moment they stood still, gaping in astonishment, and then they picked up their heels and ran, with only the bravest stealing back to peep at us in secret.

"We're not ghosts or devils," Yonit tried to reassure them, "you can go back to your bonfires."

But her voice, which for some reason sounded shaky and unnatural, only increased their fear and the uproar. As for me, the thought that now I was grown up and was making these children quake with the same kind of terror that had kept me awake at night as a kid amused me. I even laughed aloud. Yonit, on the other hand, derived no enjoyment from the scene, and my mother, wrapped in the fog that separated her from the world, shared neither in my merriment nor in Yonit's uneasiness, and she whispered in an apathetic voice, "Let's get out of here. It's time to go back."

But we stayed where we were, a few abandoned bonfires still burning around us, one of them with a pole stuck in the middle topped by a big rag doll which would soon go up in flames. On its chest was written in big, uneven letters: H-I-T-L-E-R.

My mother sat down on one of the rocks and stared at the rag doll. The expedition outside the walls of the hospital where she had been locked up for so many years was obviously having an effect on her. And Yonit, apparently saddened by the fact that the children had been forced to abandon their bonfires, waited silently to see what would happen next. Was she disturbed by her new role as some kind of devil or ghost, whose appearance frightened children out of their wits?

Now I saw the children gradually regrouping and looking with fear and longing at the wood which had been stolen from them and at the bonfires they had worked so hard to build and light. And in order to reassure them I took the basket from Yonit, removed potatoes and onions from it and laid them on the rock beside me, and tried to call the children. At this point a man appeared, presumably the father of one of the children coming to see what all the shouting was about, and approached us warily.

All of a sudden the big rag doll caught fire and collapsed. The letters spelling Hitler rose up in flames. For a moment the little wood was illuminated by a bright light, which turned our faces red.

"Yonit," said my mother suddenly, gazing dreamily at the burning doll, "thank you for coming to honor Jochanan's memory with us." And she pointed to the little tongues of flame and added, "They burned Jochanan too, they burned him in his room, not far from here. And that's how he will always be remembered."

Yonit was horrified and I raised my mother to her feet and said as cheerfully as I could, "Stop it, Mother. We came here to celebrate."

"No, my son," she said, "you know I'm not making it up. They burned your father in his room. I arrived there a few minutes after they left and all I could rescue from the fire and the firemen was that box of documents I showed you. Afterwards I went back to the hospital. Dr. Schechter would be angry if he knew I ran away. He would probably throw me out. But the main thing is that I saved the box."

And again I remembered the obscure words of the chief fireman: "You and that crazy woman in white! All you care about is your papers! She snatched the papers from the flames and went up in smoke herself."

The children came closer and closer, matching their steps to those of the man, and when they were already standing in the wood, he called out to them to carry on with what they were doing before. Most of the children returned to their bonfires and only a handful went on staring in wonder at the three alien creatures in white – us. I smiled a forced smile at them and took a few more potatoes and onions out of Yonit's basket and laid them on the rock as well.

"Take them," I said, "and let us share your bonfire. We'll sit over there on the bench, and you can call us when the potatoes and onions are ready."

I pointed the bench out to Mother and the three of us proceeded towards it.

Like three white statues we sat on the bench in the dense Jerusalem darkness which the light of the bonfires did nothing to dispel. Heavy smoke shrouded the wood and Yonit's eyes started to water. In her wildest imagination, it seemed, she could never have seen herself winding up in her present situation. Her eyes were fixed on my face, which was apparently tense, without a trace of its former exuberance. I could feel the corner of my mouth twitching. My mother sat as pale and silent as a sphinx, her white hat drooping gracelessly. I saw Yonit dropping her eyes and followed her glance, and we both saw that my mother's feet were bare. Up to now I hadn't noticed her feet, and I couldn't remember if she had left the hospital barefoot or not.

"Mother," I whispered as if continuing a conversation that had been broken off, "what were you talking about? Who set fire to Father's room? Who killed him?" There was suddenly a note of anger in my voice.

My mother kept stubbornly silent and went on staring at the bonfires which were beginning to die down.

Before long the fires had turned to piles of smoldering embers and the children poked about in them, some with sticks and some with the toes of their shoes, looking for the potatoes and onions most of which had presumably turned to coal by now. It was already late, but I still didn't want to leave the wood, which was now lit by moonlight; I had not yet given up hope that the smoke of the fires and the sparks flying in the light wind that had begun to blow would arouse my mother to speak again, to solve some part of the riddle.

A little boy and girl came up to us with three pitch-black lumps in their hands. They approached us timidly and suddenly stopped, as if alarmed by their own daring. In the end the little girl whispered, her words barely audible, "Here are two potatoes and an onion."

"Thank you," said Yonit and took a white plastic plate out of her basket. The children put their offerings on the plate and ran off.

"Mother, would you like a potato or an onion?" I asked. Her face remained blank.

She's as beautiful as a fairytale princess, as a statue, I said to myself and turned to look at Yonit, who had a slightly anxious expression on her face. I knew that sitting like this on the bench without moving or talking was difficult for her, but nevertheless, uncharacteristically, she didn't do anything to change the situation. It seemed to me that all she wanted was to help me as far as she was able.

The children began to disperse. The bonfires went out. From time to time a pair of lovers or group of youths roaming in the wood approached our bench, but they quickly retreated when they saw us. For a moment I imagined Yonit as the wicked Queen of the Night, of whom everyone was afraid, sitting here next to me looking sad but also inexplicably satisfied. Now she glanced at me again, and I tried to look calm, hoping that she was unaware of my inner agitation. The little muscle at the corner of my mouth was still twitching.

Suddenly, like a voice from the depths, we heard my mother continuing the conversation which had been cut off and which I thought would never be renewed: "I told you, didn't I? Mrs. Zilberman, the neighbor, saw them running down the stairs. They were wearing masks like gangsters. Their hands were dripping kerosene. They set fire to your father. With friends like his you don't need enemies."

"Yes," I said, stunned, and after a moment's silence I tried another tack. "Yes, Mother, you're right. Mrs. Zilberman told me the same thing. But what made you go to Daddy's room precisely on the evening when he needed you most?"

"Daddy came to see me the evening before, and for the first time in years he sat with me for hours; he simply didn't want to leave. If Dr. Schechter hadn't told him he had to let me rest he would have stayed all night. When we parted he burst into tears, hugged me and kissed me – something he hadn't done since the day you were born. And then he said goodbye and wished me well. It was clear to both of us that we would never meet again. He was hunted. Someone was threatening him."

Mother looked as exhausted as if she had been talking for hours, and as I said before, it was already late. We stood up, left the wood and climbed up Marcus Street. Later Yonit told me that it had seemed to her then that hundreds of eyes were watching us, that a Jerusalem of ghosts and supernatural powers had suddenly come alive. She couldn't even remember how we had arrived at the hospital and how we had reached my house; she was ready to believe that the meeting with my mother had never taken place, that it was all a dream. One thing we both knew for certain: the two of us spent the night together.

In the morning, when she went downstairs, neat and tidy and perfectly groomed, and made her way to the grocery shop on Azza Street, Yonit reviewed the events of the evening and night and decided, so she told me, that she was a new woman, and so she would remain for the rest of her life.

At ten o'clock in the morning, after eating breakfast, we knocked on Mrs. Zilberman's door, my father's neighbor in

Rutenberg Lane. She greeted me warmly, smiled politely at Yonit, and invited us to have a cup of tea with her. Opposite my eyes, in her modest living room, was a kitschy oil painting of leafy trees and a bubbling brook – shades of a distant Europe. Our conversation proceeded at a leisurely pace; first we talked about her children and grandchildren, then of my family, but my father was not mentioned.

I looked around and my eyes fell on an old-fashioned cupboard with glass doors standing next to the window, in an alcove in the wall. On its shelves was a spectacular collection of butterflies – each butterfly transfixed with a pin whose head matched the color of its wings.

"How beautiful and how sad they are," whispered Yonit, as if reading my thoughts.

I looked at her and for a fraction of a second I saw Ilana's face.

Mrs. Zilberman's features gradually changed too until they resembled those of the stooped old woman Ilana and I had met some years ago in the wadi behind Givat Ram. I felt a little giddy.

"Professor Zilberman loved those butterflies more than he loved me," giggled Mrs. Zilberman, and her double chin quivered.

"Yes," said Yonit, "it's a magnificent collection. It must have taken years."

I felt worse – some mysterious, irresistible force thrust me into another world, a thick fog descended and my eyes darkened. When I regained consciousness I saw Mrs. Zilberman leaning over me and holding a handkerchief soaked in eau-de-cologne to my nose, and I woke up completely.

"It will be all right," I said, trying to smile, "I feel better now."

With a winsome smile Yonit turned to reassure Mrs. Zilberman, and to me she whispered, her mouth to my ear and her breast on my shoulder, "Perhaps we should go now and come back some other time?"

But I shook my head impatiently, even dismissively, I fear, and asked Mrs. Zilberman to tell me about that fateful night when my father met his death. She responded willingly. It was evident that she had been waiting for this moment, that she was eager to share the shocking experience with someone else and lighten the load of the memory.

"I heard a strange sound from Mr. Cohen's room upstairs," she said, "and afterwards there were suspicious noises in the stairwell. I opened the door and saw two men dressed in raincoats and peculiar hats hurrying down the stairs. They gave off a strong smell of kerosene, which lingered in the air after they had gone. The tall one, who looked older, was a thin, strange-looking man, with white-framed glasses and white shoes. The other one had a frightening face, Chinese or Japanese. I didn't know what to do. I was terrified. Suddenly I smelled something burning. Then the house filled with smoke. It was coming from your father's room. I shut the door and with trembling fingers I phoned the fire department. But by the time they got here everything had burned and he was dead." Tears streamed down her cheeks and she wiped them away with a handkerchief she removed from the folds of the sofa. "I'll never forget that terrible night. I'm so sorry," she said and fell silent.

Yonit sat on the edge of her chair. Now she was the one who wanted to hear more and more details, but I wouldn't let her ask any questions. In a rage I could barely suppress I thanked Mrs. Zilberman and walked to the door. Yonit hurried after me. Slowly and heavily we descended the stairs. Yonit glanced up once or twice at the top floor where my father had lived but said nothing. When we were already walking down Radak Street she looked at me with concern, but restrained herself and left me alone.

The next three days I never left the house. Strange pictures whirled feverishly in my head, and between one picture and the next I saw Yonit's face peeping at me from different angles, in undisguised anxiety.

On the fourth day the phone rang. It was Dr. Schechter, wondering why no one had been to visit my mother. "Even Kalamaro, who has become part of the hospital landscape, has disappeared," he said in a reproachful tone.

"I'll make inquiries immediately," I said dryly and put the phone down. And then, as if in a frenzy, I began to dial. With bated breath I listened to the distant ring, and after a few seconds which seemed both to me and to Yonit like an eternity, I said frantically, in English: "Hello, Sarina *kerida*, he's disappeared, we shall never find him. How about the boy?"

"*Yo se, yo se, el tambien se desparesio!* (I know, I know, he's disappeared too)."

I nodded to her as if we were speaking face-to-face and hung up without saying goodbye.

"They've disappeared, as expected," I said, not necessarily to Yonit.

"Who, who's disappeared?"

"The boy and Kalamaro, who else?" I hurled at her as if it were her fault.

"What?!" exclaimed the startled Yonit, who had no idea of what I was talking about, and stared at me as if I had taken leave of my senses.

"I told you," I sighed impatiently, "he had enemies everywhere, in every corner of the globe. Wherever he went he was persecuted. The British, the Jews, the Arabs. And now, it turns

CHAPTER EIGHT

out, that Chinese boy too, who became Kalamaro's pawn. Who knows what mysterious forces, what sinister triads that loyal friend of the family activated in the colony in order to liquidate my father!"

Yonit sat there with her mouth open. My words sounded remote, bizarre, taken from the world of the imagination. The settling of scores because of underground activity thirty years before – could it be possible? But Kalamaro's strange, fanatical devotion to my mother made the story seem more plausible to her. She sensed that there was something unnatural here, something strange and uncanny, but nevertheless she couldn't understand how the Chinese boy had become involved in the affair. Did he know about Jochanan's connections with the Japanese and desire revenge? Did he act because of some mysterious connection with Kalamaro?

A few weeks passed, and one evening Yonit showed me a small news item in the paper which had attracted her attention. It concerned a resident of Jerusalem who found an old car without license plates somewhere in the south of the city, on the border of the Bethlehem district. He informed the police and they opened an investigation. When they failed to come up with anything at the end of the period stipulated by law, the finder's lawyers demanded that the police hand over the car to him. The item struck Yonit as curious ("Someone finds a car as if it's a watch fallen off somebody's wrist?") and so she showed it to me. I read it again and again. There's one little detail here, I said to myself, that Yonit didn't notice: the car was a brown 1948 Morris Minor. I cut out the item and added it to the crammed file holding my father's notes and papers. Then I tied it up neatly and put it away in the suitcase in the storage space under the bathroom ceiling. The affair of my father's life and death is concluded, I said to myself as I climbed down the ladder, but my own life is going nowhere.

I was confused and disturbed, exhausted by everything that had happened, and I wanted very much to open a new chapter in my life, a chapter that would be all my own.

"Why don't we go out tonight?" I said without any preamble to Yonit, who was standing at the sink in the kitchen. "How would you like to go to the movies?"

"Good idea. Why not?"

Chapter Nine

Like a strange, foreign royal couple Sarina and Leonardo arrived in the country. The heavy, intricately carved antique chests they had brought with them were enough to attract the attention of the passersby in the quiet Rechavia street. The chests contained fine cushions and quilts, exquisitely woven mats, rare embroidery and all kinds of household goods: expensive sets of dishes from south and north China, wood and bamboo screens, and furnishings that had given rise to admiration even in the distant colony full of chinoiserie. Carefully packed garments too, of every kind and color, arrived in the two trucks parked on the pavement. Among the items were buried Ming vases, ancient jars, lacquered boxes and colorful glass and ceramic articles. The "Greek chest" that Bracha and Adina had sent to Hong Kong from Ioannina wound up here too. Pictures in magnificent frames brought strange and distant landscapes to the Holy City: the bustling bay of Hong Kong, the harbor city of Shanghai in the thirties, on the eve of the World War, the Gobi Desert and the mountain ranges on the Greek border with Albania, and an ancient map of the Middle East with Latin names and gold chains around its edges...

I, of course, was the chief organizer of the "royal event" – as I called the operation of bringing them to Israel. I rented a spacious apartment in Balfour Street, otherwise known as the "street of the consulates," for my aunt and her benefactor, not far from my own home. It was a large apartment dating from the British Mandate, designed for the residence of a foreign ambassador. On the day my aunt Sarina arrived in Jerusalem there were flags flying from a number of roofs and balconies, just as they had flown many years before when a distant relative of my father's was here on a visit from Egypt, and I was brought to see her. This play has already been staged in the street of the consulates once before, I said to myself – and now that I came to think of it, wasn't the house I had found for Aunt Sarina the same house I had entered then, in short pants and suspenders, when I was five or six years old?

A few days after his arrival Leonardo fixed a tall pole to the balcony of their apartment and proudly flew from it an unfamiliar flag – the flag of an Asian republic which he was representing as an honorary consul. He bought a big new car too and parked it proudly in the spot officially allocated it, and on the consular license plates a local artist painted the flag of the distant republic, unrecognizable to any of the passersby. How perfectly matched the notions of consul and Jerusalem seemed in this street! Sarina seemed close to Jerusalem too, despite years and generations of estrangement.

Sarina told me that in the days following our brief telephone conversation she had been full of fear. Sometimes it seemed to her that the disappearance of Kalamaro and the boy had upset some cosmic balance which had been maintained until that moment. Again and again she looked at Leonardo's cupboard of stuffed birds, where the dust was gathering on the shelves. And one morning when she was wandering around the apartment, her eyes straying continuously to the cupboard, she was seized by a terrible agitation: one of the birds, a medium-sized black eagle, had moved slightly towards the glass door as if intent on breaking out.

Leonardo, she said, was very withdrawn and remote in those days. When he left for the office in the morning his face would vanish from her memory and be replaced by the delicate features of Hans, the German officer who had saved her family during the war. The Land of Israel, too, filled her thoughts. If I don't go now, when I'm almost sixty, she said to herself, I never will. And one morning she made a vow that by the following Yom Kippur she would be living in Jerusalem. And she kept her vow. In the autumn of 1972, shortly before Rosh Hashana, she arrived in Jerusalem to settle there for good.

Every Friday night I would be invited to dinner with Sarina and Leonardo, and sometimes I would bring Yonit with me. These festive dinners gave me a feeling of family life which I had not known since childhood. They were very different from our family meals at home, but at the same time they reminded me of distant things that made me happy. Leonardo would fill our glasses with the fine wines he had brought with him from Hong Kong, and after the rich meal he would offer me a cigar and a glass of excellent brandy, press me to drink, and add, "One day you and I will do business together."

Yonit continued to pursue her studies. And after the day's work in the department laboratory, she would often drop in to the Reil home to enjoy the cosy atmosphere. She would have long talks with Sarina while Leonardo and I conferred in his study.

The only one who lost out as a result of the new developments was my mother, something for which I frequently castigated myself, but did nothing to amend. Every now and then Dr. Schechter phoned me to complain about my lack of interest in his patient. "Why don't you take your mother out for a walk again?" he urged me. But I was completely absorbed in my work with Leonardo, and the little free time I had I devoted to Yonit. My visits to the hospital became more and more infrequent. Many days would pass without my seeing her, and only the pressure exerted by Yonit, with her graphic descriptions of Mother's (this was how she had begun to refer to her) loneliness, would jolt me out of my apathy and send me down Disraeli Street to knock on the big iron gates.

I sometime played with the idea of bringing her with us to Sarina's house on a Friday night, but I always drew back at the last minute. I was afraid that a visit from her would disrupt the idyll I was so desperate to preserve. Though Sarina never discussed my mother with me, it was obvious that she was afraid of meeting her sick sister-in-law. The thought of visiting the closed institution, too, made her shudder. In her mind's eye she saw some imaginary Irena (she had never actually seen my mother) sitting locked up in a hiding place in Ioannina during the Nazi occupation, and the horrors of the war, which she had been fortunate enough to survive, came back to haunt her. Here in Jerusalem she sought peace of mind, rest after everything she had been through. She had made a number of good friends in the few months since their arrival in Jerusalem, found a place in the social life of Rechavia among women of her own age, many of them widows, and was reluctant to embark on any new adventures. Even the one visit she had paid to her brother Jochanan's grave had affected her severely, and for days afterwards she had been too upset to talk, causing Leonardo some concern.

CHAPTER NINE

One Friday night I suggested to Sarina and Leonardo that they should throw a big party to celebrate the anniversary of their coming to Jerusalem. At first Sarina was alarmed and rejected the idea outright, but gradually her opposition died down. Yonit, who helped me to persuade her, suggested that the party be in honor of my thirtieth birthday too. Now I was the reluctant one, but the fact that it was Yonit who had suggested it and that it meant so much to her moved me greatly and made it difficult for me to refuse.

We went on discussing the details of the party and Yonit stood up and left the room. After a while we heard her suddenly crying out from the hallway: "I don't want to lose the child!"

We hurried to her in alarm and found her kneeling on the floor, her face pale and anguished. I went up and knelt beside her, and since I did not know what else to do I kissed her and murmured "Yonit, dear little Yonit." And when she saw me like this she seemed to suddenly recover and a shy, embarrassed smile appeared on her lips. "I'm all right, don't worry," she whispered.

I helped her up, and holding her in a tender embrace led her to an armchair in the living room. I tried to guess what had happened to her and all kinds of wild conjectures passed through my mind, until I suddenly remembered the words she had cried out in the hallway and a light dawned in my eyes: "What's this, another reason to celebrate?" I whispered in her ear.

One afternoon I found Yonit sprawled out on our bed.
"What's wrong?" I asked.
She turned her face towards me but said nothing.

"What happened to you, my little dove? What are you doing here, didn't you have an appointment with your supervisor about a research project?"

"I didn't go," she said in a defiant tone. "I went for a walk in Independence Park instead." She went on to say that her studies and connections to the academic world now seemed meaningless to her. When she was in the park she sat on a bench and thought of "the little things that make life worthwhile." She watched two children playing in the sand pit and on the jungle gym, the mothers keenly debating the relative merits of various washing machines while keeping a vigilant eye on their children digging in the sand.

"Nearby, on the lawn," she said excitedly, "a group of Arab youths were sitting in a circle. In the middle of the circle stood a huge, gleaming transistor radio. The Oriental tunes blaring from it swept me up into a colorful, sensuous world, as bright as the shirts of the young men accompanying the singer who seemed to be hidden inside the radio. And when the rays of the sun struck the radio in a burst of dazzling light I felt an impulse to leap into the middle of the circle and break into song, perhaps even to dance, to join them in their celebration, but my stomach turned over and a great weakness overcame me. I sat there limp as a rag, with my legs slightly parted, and waited for the weakness to pass. An old man in a grey hat, dragging a tiny, rat-sized dog, walked past, and I remembered Leonardo and the plans for the party, and then I thought of you again. What are you up to? Why did you hesitate when I suggested that the party be in honor of your birthday, too, and why did you suddenly agree with that strange smile of yours all over your face...."

"Never mind the party," I said, "the main thing is that you feel better."

"Yes," she said absentmindedly and went on with her story. "One of the Arabs sitting in the circle kept staring at me. In the end he stood up, brushed the grass off his trousers, and approached the bench. I tried to ignore him. The youths seemed to me like children, wrapped up in themselves and out of touch with reality. At that moment I felt like reality itself, a reality impossible to ignore. He looked straight into my face, but I wasn't afraid.

"He stood there facing me, a few steps away, took a cigarette out of his shirt pocket, lit it and blew the smoke at me. I heard the signal announcing the news in Arabic coming from the transistor, but believe me the signals from my belly sounded a lot clearer and more emphatic. Again I thought of you, of the 'Destruction of the Third Temple' that you're always talking about, about your hatred for Golda Meir and her government, who in my opinion are doing the best they can.

"And then the lad asked me in fluent Hebrew, 'What's your opinion of the situation?' I said nothing. 'Let's see what the results of your elections are,' he went on. He spoke rather arrogantly, even threateningly, and I began to feel a little frightened. I wanted to get up and go away but my legs failed me. I couldn't move. I looked straight into his eyes and I saw a kind of curiosity which when I didn't react turned into undisguised loathing. I ignored him and looked at the two tots playing in the sandpit, whose mouths were already full of sand. Now they were quarreling violently, and suddenly they began to cry, their tears streaking their dirty faces. Their mothers hurried up and led them away from the playground like little prisoners, to the main path crossing the park and then home. When I turned back to the swaggering youth confronting me, he was already on his way back to his friends, making a rude gesture which caused them to bellow with ugly laughter. The woman on the radio sang loudly and the youths clapped in time. After a while I stood up, feeling heavy and weak and giddy, and came here and fell straight into bed."

"You have a good rest," I said.

She turned onto her side and motioned me to sit down next to her, saying in a whisper, "Come here."

"What's going to happen now?" she asked and patted her belly.

"It's definite, right?" I asked.

"Yes, it's definite."

"That's great," I said, but I knew very well that Yonit had seen the cloud crossing my face.

Chapter Ten

"The party of the year" was set for Tuesday, the second of October 1973. I spent a lot of time making preparations and taking care of all the details.

"We're celebrating three occasions," I said to Yonit, "the anniversary of the Reils' arrival in Jerusalem, my thirtieth birthday (if you insist) and of course our marriage. Our wedding will be a day to remember."

I looked straight into her eyes, suppressing my excitement and waiting for her reaction. But she didn't say a word. My announcement did not surprise her. She knew me better than I imagined. And nevertheless her silence disappointed me, and I went on eagerly, swept away by my plans: "Nobody, not even Sarina and Leonardo, will know in advance about the wedding. Just imagine!" I felt like an actor on a stage where someone had put me against my will. "And then, during the course of the evening, before the royal refreshments are served, I'll bring out some little rabbi from the room at the end of the hallway, and when all the guests think he's a conjurer come to pull rabbits out of his hat, he'll set up an embroidered wedding canopy on decorated poles – and the ceremony will commence!"

A strange idea, as I admitted to myself, but Yonit did not protest. It appeared that she had grown accustomed to my eccentricities and caprices. And perhaps it was her swelling belly that had taken away her will to resist? In any case it was clear that she too was swept up in the enthusiasm which had taken control of me and which surprised even me by its intensity. Sometimes it seemed to me that forces beyond my comprehension had taken me over and were directing my actions. And Yonit too, apparently sensed that I would still do many exceptional things, and the wedding was only the beginning of a brilliant new chapter in my life. From occasional remarks she made it clear that she believed with all her heart that after the wedding everything would look different, and that the future was full of promise.

Dressed up to the nines, the guests arrived for the party. The invitations they had received were unique in their form, style and language: long shiny cards, folded in two, with each page devoted to one of the four languages in which the invitation was written: Hebrew, English, Greek and Ladino.

"Sarina and Leonardo's first year in Jerusalem" was written in large letters at the head of each page. And below, on a separate line: "Please join us in our celebration," and at the bottom, after details of the time and place, came our joint signatures – mine and Yonit's.

Sarina's friends were astonished by the diversity of the many guests assembled at the Reil home that night. Someone was overheard to say that such a human mélange had not been seen in Jerusalem since the beginning of the British Mandate, and someone else responded to this remark by calling it an understatement, and declaring that the city had never seen anything like it before.

And indeed, only a few of the guests knew each other – a most unusual phenomenon in a place like Jerusalem. I had invested a lot of thought in compiling the invitation list, which, apart from Sarina's and Leonardo's friends, included everyone I regarded as having contributed in one way or another to the formation of my character at the different stages of my life, everyone I bore a part of inside me.

My mother was the first to arrive. She was, of course, wearing a white dress and a hat with a white ribbon, and flat white shoes which looked a little odd to those used to seeing her barefoot. Her skin was smooth and even browner than usual, as if she had spent hours getting a tan on the beach. It seemed to me that she had made a special effort to display her beauty, and she looked like a movie star who had dropped into the reality of Jerusalem straight from the screen of the Zion Cinema. She was accompanied by Dr. Schechter, his plump body squeezed into an old-fashioned striped suit, and his hair smoothly combed.

Distant Hong Kong was represented by George Woodhead; he had been in London on a business trip and was about to return to the Far East, and he was obviously pleased to have received an invitation to a party in honor of his friend Leonardo. He had never understood what had possessed him to leave the colony and settle in Palestine, and the meeting with me, Jochanan's son, only increased his curiosity as to the fate of the country under Jewish rule.

Woodhead's secretary, who accompanied him, stood out sharply in the crowd. Her slanting eyes shone, there was a winning smile on her face, and the stern efficiency of her office persona had vanished without a trace. Her plunging neckline and exotic beauty attracted general attention the moment she stepped into the room. And she, who until meeting me in the colony had hardly been aware of Israel's existence, walked about as if in a dream. She quickly found someone to talk to – the black professor Arno Jackson, a biologist from Princeton who was on sabbatical at Hebrew University, with whom Yonit had become acquainted while conducting her research. Jackson was an energetic man, full of vitality and humor. We had already invited him to our home on a number of occasions and spent a few evenings together at the Little Gallery, a popular Jerusalem café with an artistic, bohemian atmosphere. Jackson liked the Gallery and made friends with a number of the regulars.

A jazz fan who seemed to enjoy social gatherings of all kinds, he attached himself to Mr. Woodhead's beautiful secretary as soon as he set eyes on her and stuck to her like a leech, smiling constantly and showing his gleaming teeth.

The guests were now joined by three veterans from the underground, Spielberg among them. I didn't believe I would succeed in bringing them here, but my promise that they would find rare "human material" with a direct bearing on the history of the underground had apparently had its effect. Spielberg, who was busy writing a history of the group at the time, and energetically pursuing additional sources to the ones already in his possession, did not decline my invitation outright, and even showed a certain interest. In my telephone conversation with him I struck a sentimental chord, and Spielberg (the man with the heart of stone) did not sound indifferent to it. Perhaps he had mellowed with the years, I said to myself, and argued fervently: "After all the rejections, refusals and humiliations you people have handed out to me, it seems to me that five years after his death, you owe me, as Jochanan's son, the honor of accepting my invitation to be present at an occasion of great significance to me."

Spielberg muttered something in his distant home near Tel Aviv, but his words did not reach me in Jerusalem.

"After my father was murdered," I continued and paused for a moment in the vain hope that Spielberg would react to this pronouncement, "he's entitled to some sign that his old comrades have not abandoned him completely, at least not on a day of such importance to his son!" I was careful to address Spielberg in the plural, since in my opinion he was not a single individual but the representative of a shadowy clique which had played an important part in my father's life, and perhaps also in his death.

CHAPTER TEN

"What's so important about this party of yours?" Spielberg finally asked.

"I'm getting married," I unwillingly disclosed, and smiled bitterly to myself: now Spielberg of all people knew the secret which would come as such a surprise to everybody else, including the parents of the young couple. And this unwitting little triumph on his part caused me some displeasure.

And indeed Spielberg did not come alone – two grey, elderly men I did not know came with him and stayed close to him all evening, not letting him out of their sight. It was hard to tell if he was their prisoner and they his warders, or if he was their master and they his servants. Wherever the three of them went in the spacious living room they gave off a smell of naphthalene, increasing the air of mystery in which they were wrapped. One of Spielberg's companions was short and sturdy, with a sly, stubborn face. When I stood next to him I felt an absolute certainty that this man had been closely connected to my father's affair, and that he would have clear answers to many of the questions that troubled me. If only I could get this dwarfish sphinx to talk!

Mrs. Zilberman came too. She was the only one who brought a modest gift, although it was presumably not quite clear to her for whom it was intended. It was a delicately carved little wooden box with a glass lid holding six exquisite butterflies. In each corner of the box lay a glittering mothball. When she walked in she immediately noticed my mother and she ran up to her and kissed her as if she were her long-lost sister, and put the butterfly box in her hands. My mother, who was more lucid than she had been for many years, conversed with her at length, until Sarina interrupted them to lead my mother to a corner of the room, where she plied her with sweet drinks and showered her with questions. I was sorry I couldn't hear what they were saying.

The owner of my favorite restaurant in the Machane Yehuda market, a bald, thin young man with a sickly appearance, appeared in the doorway with his plump wife, whose hand he kept hold of as they stood among the guests. My two previous girlfriends arrived with their husbands; neither of them knew about the other's existence, and both of them were strangers to Yonit.

Yonit's mother and father came a little late, explaining their tardiness by a problem with the car, and pointing to the door, where her brother immediately appeared in a lieutenant colonel's uniform. Yonit fell on their necks with kisses. When she embraced her mother tears streamed down her cheeks. Her mother seemed astonished at this public display of affection on the part of her daughter.

A number of foreign consuls, colleagues of Leonardo's, gathered around the grand piano, whispering in Spanish, occasionally greeting a new arrival with cheers and inviting him to drink a toast with them.

Four musicians played waltzes, and I overheard someone say that the Congress of Vienna was apparently not yet over, it had simply been transferred to Jerusalem.

Uniformed waiters circulated among the guests bearing gleaming trays laden with drinks, tiny exotic sandwiches, little pastries and stuffed dates that melted in the mouth.

All my plans were carried out to the letter. Only the unprofessional usher I borrowed from the King David Hotel – a silver-haired butler from the days of the Mandate – immediately abandoned his post for the charms of a heavily made up middle-aged Greek woman, whose identity was known to me alone. Once in a while he would go reluctantly to the door and justify his presence by calling out the name of the new arrival: "Elyakim Levy, Doctor." "Amitzur Dan, Dean."

When the plumber Moshe arrived, a devoted fan of the Beitar Jerusalem football team whom I met at regular intervals in the Pinati Restaurant after serving with him for years in the reserves, he was announced simply as "Moshe." Two students from my year at the university (the only year during which I had devoted most of my time to studying) arrived next and took up their positions near George Woodhead, to whom nobody was paying any attention. They tried to find something to talk about and Danny, second in command of a reserves battalion, was delighted to discover that the elderly Englishman had a military past. Eli, the corporal, who had recently been promoted to the post of junior officer in his computer unit, listened rather shamefacedly to the conversation. All his attempts to take part in the "majors' conversation," as he said later, were in vain.

Yonit looked beautiful and mature. She circulated easily among the guests, like a practiced hostess, exchanging a few remarks with one, smiling at another, and urging a third to taste the refreshments. When I glanced at her from time to time it seemed to me that her rounding belly was bulging out of her white dress, and I felt a little embarrassed.

Past and present mingled in the Reils' spacious living room. Only the future was shrouded in fog. The decor, the babble of languages, and the faces of the guests reinforced my feeling that I was living an event from the past in which I played only a very small part. I reflected on the period before the departure of the British from the country, which I loved reading about and which Kalamaro talked about so much. How proud he would have been to be with us tonight, I said to myself, and suddenly I could have sworn that Kalamaro was indeed present, hovering about the room. I sensed his presence clearly, and I asked myself again (as I had frequently asked myself lately) how I could be so forgiving towards the man who had killed my father.

I shook off these reflections, surveyed the assembled guests with satisfaction, and decided that the time had come to introduce Woodhead to the "Spielbergs" as I called the grey trio to myself. I immediately bore down on the Hong Kong businessman in order to take him away from Danny and Eli, but on the way, in the melee of hands, faces and voices, I bumped into the gatekeeper of my mother's hospital, Mr. Levy, dragging his small, wrinkled, sheepish wife behind him.

"I feel as if I'm at work here," he sniggered.

"Tell me," I pressed him, "do you also feel that Kalamaro should have been here tonight?"

"What are you talking about?! He is here!" pronounced the gatekeeper decisively. "I'm sure he's here."

And then my father's old aunt appeared in the doorway, Aunt Sultana's wrinkled sister. I hurried up gladly to greet her, kissed her on both hairy cheeks, and thought I could detect a distant scent of moldy sweets. The lines my father had written about his childhood came back to me. And as I was looking into her shrunken, wrinkled face I saw behind her shoulder the tall, erect and aristocratic figure of Lord Mansfield, founder of the eye hospital in Oxfordshire and now a visiting professor at Hadassah Hospital in Ein Kerem. He served with Woodhead during the war. He bowed and apologized for coming late.

"I only returned from London late last night," he explained, "from a meeting in the House of Lords."

The disappointing usher was absorbed in conversation with the Greek woman again, and once more he had missed the entrance of a guest, this time one with an imposing appearance and title. When he realized his mistake, too late, he turned pale, and then marched to the door with his back stiff as a ramrod, in case additional members of the House of Lords put in an appearance.

I wanted to find Levy the gatekeeper again and hear more about Kalamaro, but then my eyes fell on the little figure of Mazal Kastilia standing shyly at the door and not knowing where to turn.

"I went to see her again in her poor hut," wrote Jochanan in his diary, "she was lying in bed, her appearance sickly and the furrows of age etched deeply on her face. Her chest was sunken and the covers of her bed dragged on the damp yellowish floor. 'I have to ask you for your blessing before setting out on a long journey,' I said to her...."

For years Mazal had worked as a maid in the house of the Matarsso family, but I was unable to discover the roots of the deep attachment my father felt towards her. At the same time, I knew that I had to invite her to the party, that there was a part of her, too, in me. I ran up to greet her and led her gently to an armchair next to the buffet.

While I was in the act of offering her a glass of grapefruit juice, my heart began to beat faster as my eye fell on Hannah, my third-grade teacher. How beautiful she had been then, and how I had adored her. One day when I was disturbing the lesson she sent me out of the class in disgrace. I wandered around the big, cold stone building, beside myself with sorrow and remorse. In the end I knelt down on the hallway floor and began to daydream – my usual refuge in times of stress. And all the time I heard the sound of her voice coming from the classroom whose door had been shut against me. The pupils were told to read something and summarize it in silence, and then I heard the creaking hinges of the door opening. I tensed. Hannah emerged from the classroom and made for the lavatory.

Out of the corner of my downcast eyes I saw her shapely legs as she walked past me, ignoring my disgraced existence. Later I heard the sound of the water flushing, the lavatory door opened and Hannah turned towards the staff room. The moments of silence and suspense that followed I shall never forget.

"Benhazar, come here, please," at last I heard my teacher's voice. The "please" at the end of the sentence was a command not to be disobeyed.

I stood up and with my head hanging walked like a condemned man to the place of execution. The staff room was empty. There were a lot of chairs standing around the heavy brown table, but Hannah instructed me to sit on the cold floor at her feet. I stared at her knees, and listened to her scolding through a dense fog, but the cuts of the cane on my back I felt sharply enough – a sensation I had never felt before. Years later, during my military service, in the long hours of guard duty in the infinite dark of the night, in ambushes on cold, rainy days, when fear threatened to overwhelm me, I often remembered that occasion in the staff room – sitting with my back bowed, my hands between my knees.

And here was Hannah herself, twenty-two years older, kissing me on the cheek as I closed my eyes.

"What's happening here?" she asked sweetly.

"We're celebrating a number of family events," I replied with a mysterious smile.

The time had come to begin the program. I stepped up onto the little platform next to the musicians, and hushed the audience. Then I delivered a prepared speech, in English.

"Mother, Lord Mansfield, dear guests, thank you all for coming here today to be present at a threefold celebration. First, the anniversary of Sarina's and Leonardo's aliyah to the Holy Land. Sarina comes from an ancient family with its roots in the Land of Israel. For years she has wandered the wide world, known hardship during the Nazi occupation of Greece, and now at last she has returned to us, to her rightful place, to her origins. And with her, her dear companion, Leonardo. If I were to recount the history and deeds of this noble couple to you we would be here all night, and so I will say only this: their love and concern for one another is the subject for a fascinating book, not an improvised speech. Let us wish them many more happy years here, in Jerusalem. And now let's raise our glasses in a toast – to Leonardo and Sarina!"

The room resounded to cries of "Lechayim!"

"Secondly," I raised my voice to make myself heard over the noise which refused to die down, "at the request of Yonit let me say that today is my thirtieth birthday. For some reason she considers this a landmark, even though I find it difficult to agree with her, especially as I stand here before so many people whose lives were and are so much more remarkable than mine, dear friends who have done so much for the general good in days of peace and of war, more than I could ever hope to do in all the years remaining to me. And therefore let me propose a toast to you, my dear friends and relatives."

And again I raised my glass, took a sip, and continued: "And now, since I never made a speech on the occasion of my bar mitzvah, in October 1956, whose celebration was cancelled owing to the Suez Campaign, I will say a few belated words which should have been said then: I will thank my dear mother, Irena, standing here among us, and wish her a good, healthy, happy life…"

My face beamed and my mother, trying to hide in a corner, blushed. Everyone smiled.

"And now let me remember my father Jochanan, whom many of you knew better than I ever did. My father dedicated his life to his country, and it could even be said that he sacrificed himself on its altar. He was a sensitive and original man. His letters, his notes, his articles and lectures, many of which burned in the fire that consumed him too in its flames, express what he wished to bequeath to the generations to come. Father believed that the enemy had to be defeated at all costs, without concessions, without negotiations. In order to destroy the enemy any alliance was legitimate in his eyes, even with those who may have seemed more terrible than the enemy himself. My father believed, as many of you know, that any foreign power occupying our country, restricting our freedom and sovereignty, had to be fought to the bitter end, come what may. Whereas ordinary anti-Semites, as long as they had no designs on the land – even the worst of them, even Hitler himself – with such people it was possible and legitimate to negotiate and even to make alliances, if necessary, in order to ensure the success of the struggle against the foreign occupier.

"At first glance, and so it was seen by many, there is a terrible and irreconcilable contradiction here. But I believe in the logic of this position, which required rapid tactical change in the light of the prevailing situation, movement at all costs, since maintaining momentum in the struggle to break out of the historical circumstances in which we were trapped was a positive response to the situation, whereas resignation and adjustment meant treading in the same spot, and in fact, retreat.

"My father's path was severely criticized, as we all know, but I still believe today that worse than all the criticism leveled at him from outside was the intolerance displayed towards him by his own comrades, who in spite of the persecution they themselves suffered at the hands of the British and the Jewish establishment, showed no understanding for his original ideas regarding collaboration with Japan, the rising power in Asia at the time, and stubbornly resisted his practical initiatives in this area."

As I spoke I looked around for the "Spielbergs" but I couldn't see them. They must be hiding somewhere behind the piano, I said to myself in disappointment, and I went on: "I won't go into the details of my father's hopes and plans here, or try to estimate their chances of being realized after the event, but I think I would be right in saying that the roots of the criticism against him lay in the arrogant self-confidence of his opponents and their pretensions to know what the future would bring. I find it difficult to accept that in the rapidly changing conditions existing during that war, conditions that were impossible to predict, any strategy should have been ruled out in advance. As the French say, '*à la guerre comme à la guerre.*' Let's not forget that even Herzl negotiated with the anti-Semite von Plehve, who was responsible for the Kishinev pogrom. As far as the Japanese are concerned, can anyone seriously argue that they were anti-Semites? Should my father's ideas have been rejected out of hand? Certainly not in the conditions prevailing then in Palestine. Things looked so bad under Mandatory rule that almost any alternative would have been preferable.

"And nevertheless, my friends, nevertheless, ladies and gentlemen, I don't believe in absolute victory, just as I don't believe in crushing defeat. And in this I differ from the concept represented by my father. The defeated today can be the victor tomorrow, and he who hurries to celebrate his victory today may find himself defeated tomorrow. Over there, in East Asia, on which my father pinned his hopes, this is a fact that is known and even enshrined in writing. But unfortunately the same cannot be said of us here. The Chinese character for war (used also in Japan) is composed of two parts: the upper part represents the spear thrusting forward, and the lower part signifies restraint and prevention. The Chinese in their wisdom saw that war contains within it the possibility of peace. The belief in absolute victory is weakness, just as winning absolutely is losing. I sense that in the days to come we will be put to a harsh test and we would do well to remember these things. Only a draw, or a delicate balance between the opposing sides, holds out a chance of success. It is possible, of course, to argue that anyone advocating this idea is not as great a patriot as those who call for the crushing of the enemy to dust, but I beg to differ. Precisely when our enemies regain their confidence and self-respect, they will be ready to negotiate with us, and then perhaps we will reach the peace we long for.

"Recently, as some of you know, I embarked on a feverish search for my father and made quite a nuisance of myself with several of those present, in the process. To my regret I cannot tell you today that I found him or that I got to the bottom of his personality. After he died I felt an urgent need to know more about him, and from the fragments that I discovered I tried to construct a full picture, but I failed. Today I am in possession of somewhat larger parts of the puzzle, but the work is not yet over and I doubt if I will ever be able to finish it. And now I must look to my own future.

"Each of the six years that have passed since the last round between us and our Arab neighbors and my father's death was as hard as a number of years for me. Biologically I may be thirty, but I feel far older...at least thirty-six. When he turned thirty-six Lord Byron wrote a poem that has gone on echoing inside me ever since my schooldays. It was my beloved teacher Max Peterson, who is not with us tonight, who first read this poem aloud to me. And with your permission I will now read to you the first and last two verses of the poem by the great Romantic, which express so well my feelings today:

'Tis time this heart should be unmoved,
Since others it hath ceased to move:
Yet, though I cannot be beloved,
Still let me love!

My days are in the yellow leaf;
The flowers and fruits of love are gone;
The worm, the canker, and the grief
Are mine alone!

[...]

If thou regrett'st thy youth, *why live?*
The land of honourable death
Is here – up to the field, and give
Away thy breath!

Seek out – less often sought than found –
A soldier's grave, for thee the best;
Then look around, and choose thy ground,
And take thy rest."*

Here I fell silent for a moment. Next to the window stood George Woodhead, his face pale and his glass trembling in his hand. It was clear to me that he – perhaps alone among the guests – knew that the poem had been written in Missolonghi in Greece only three months before the death of Byron, who was already tired of living and who, more than seeking to liberate Greece, wanted to die in it. It was his last poem. I looked at Woodhead and smiled, but my heart was sad; I even felt a little sick.

---

* "On This Day I Complete My Thirty-sixth Year," *The Poetical Works of Lord Byron* (London: Oxford University Press/Humphrey Milford, 1933).

"Today I complete my thirtieth year, and I have no glad tidings to bring you. A great storm is ahead of us, and it is too late to change the course of events, too late to correct our mistakes.

"Many of you, each in his own way, have played a part in my life. Without you I would not be what I am today, for good or ill. Allow me, therefore, to present each of you with a modest gift – a coin minted specially for this occasion. On one side is a view of a corner of this city, which is a part of me, and on the other the words 'For being a part of the landscape of my life.'"

I was very moved and for a short time, which seemed to me an eternity, I said nothing. There was not a sound to be heard in the big room. In this silence I concluded my speech: "The third reason for our being gathered here tonight will be made known to you in a moment, and it will clarify that delicate balance which seems so crucial to me. There is no evil without good, 'from strength came forth sweetness,' as it says in the Bible, or if you will, '*yin* and *yang*,' as the Chinese say. The rather harsh words I had to say here require something to balance and correct them. I call upon Rabbi Shlomo Nissim to enter and conduct the next part of this festive occasion."

The guests were astonished. Some of them realized immediately what was afoot, others seemed dazed by all the words still echoing in the air and bewildered by their conclusion. The rabbi emerged from the little room at the end of the hallway, carrying the rolled-up canopy and poles. He was beaming with happiness and it was clear that he had not heard (or had not understood) my words or grasped my intention. Like a professional actor he mounted the little platform with an agile step, erected the canopy and called on "the virtuous maid Yonit, of the house of Harmelech" to come forth. The guests made way and Yonit, dragging her bewildered parents behind her, stepped into the center of attention. Then the rabbi beckoned me and I too approached the platform. He whispered some banal joke in my ear and began reading in a low voice. At the words "the voice of the groom and the voice of the bride, the voice of joy and the voice of mirth" he raised his voice. My mother approached the canopy and silence fell, broken only by the muffled sobs of Yonit's mother.

When the ceremony was over the guests broke up into little groups again and stood eating and drinking while Yonit and I circulated among them. At midnight everybody went home, taking their leave of us in a shower of good wishes. My mother too left for the hospital, accompanied by Dr. Schechter. Before she left she kissed me, an expression of boundless joy in her beautiful big eyes. At that moment, there was no doubt of her lucidity and her happiness.

The only people left in the large living room were Yonit's parents and brother, Sarina and Leonardo, and us, the young couple. After some slightly forced laughter to break the ice, we began to discuss "various things that needed to be taken care of," in the words of Mr. Harmelech, who had barely recovered from the "unfair surprise" that his daughter had prepared for him and his wife. It was obvious that it cost him an effort to refrain from spoiling what Yonit referred to as "the most beautiful and sincere evening of my life," and turn with no more ado to the business in which his past as a trade-union negotiator made him an expert – a discussion of the "economic future" of the newlyweds.

Now Leonardo assumed the main role. In a patriarchal style which seemed to me to include expressions from the world of the Chinese warlords, he promised his "full protection" to the two young people. And when he saw the look on the faces of Yonit's parents and brother, he immediately added that he wasn't talking about favors but rights.

"I'm a businessman," he said, "and I assure you that every cent this young man gets from me will be honestly earned by his work for my company."

And he went on to say that he intended to promote me in the company and gradually transfer authority to me according to my talents and capabilities, referring discreetly to his childless state and his hopes that the bonds between us would grow closer and that in the course of time we would be like father and son.

At half past two in the morning Mr. Harmelech was exhausted but reassured as to the material prospects of his daughter. As they were getting ready to leave, however, he demanded to be allowed to pay his share of the wedding expenses. And when Leonardo politely but firmly refused his offer, Mr. Harmelech appeared to be offended to the depths of his soul. This unexpected last-minute crisis was resolved by Sarina in her sensible way. She justified the bride's father and promised him that within a week he would receive a detailed account of which he would be requested to pay half on terms convenient to him.

"He is certainly entitled to participate in the expenses," she concluded and silenced Leonardo with a look.

Epilogue

Benhazar and Yonit had only four days of peace. On Yom Kippur war broke out and he was called up. Once and once only Yonit received regards from "somewhere in the south," as the anonymous voice, apparently a soldier from his battalion, whispered over the phone. Afterwards came long days without a word.

Even when soldiers began coming to town on brief leaves, and it was clear that it was quiet on the southern front, Yonit heard nothing from Benhazar. She started going every day to the office of the major in charge of the city, which was always crowded with soldiers' families. Tense and worried, people from all walks of life waited in front of the little window, where a young female soldier appeared from time to time, the gravity of her task evident on her face. From time to time the door of the inner office opened and deputations left on their way to the homes of the missing, the prisoners, the wounded and the dead.

One morning, when Yonit finally succeeded in reaching the window and meeting the eyes of the young soldier, she realized that she was unable to provide her with a single detail to identify Benhazar the soldier: she didn't know his serial number, his rank or the military mail number from which his call-up order had been sent. A few days later she found herself attracting unusual attention. At first she felt a certain relief, but gradually she began to suspect that the warmth of her reception was a means of preparing her for bad news. At first they told her that because of the unclear situation and the chaos prevailing in the battlefields next to the canal, they did not want to mislead her by giving her unconfirmed information.

"We would like to hope," explained a young officer in a friendly tone, "that your husband joined up with another unit in the course of the fighting, a detail that has not yet been reported. On the other hand, he might be missing."

Yonit declined to go into the subtle difference between these military definitions.

But a few days later she was officially informed that "Corporal Benhazar Cohen has not been located among the fallen or the wounded. The possibility that he has been taken prisoner by the Egyptians is also unlikely."

Afterwards he was declared missing in action.

Inquiries made in his unit came up with nothing. No new hypotheses were put forward, and no basis was found for reinvestigating the old ones. Nobody was able to say exactly when and how contact with Benhazar had been lost.

Yonit sat for hours with his friends and commanding officers, who told her that as far as they remembered he was last seen leaving "South Clutch" for "Graveyard" to take over from a guard posted next to an anti-aircraft battery – but he never got there. A heavy Egyptian barrage had caused chaos in the Israeli lines, and Benhazar had apparently been among the casualties. But he had not been found among the evacuated. It was as if the earth had swallowed him up. The names coined for the places, the initials and the military terms with which the soldiers peppered their words meant nothing to Yonit, and only increased her feelings of alienation and fear. Their whispered confabulations when she left the room for a moment to go to the kitchen or the other room deepened her anxiety even more. Most of the time she sat still and silent, as if she had been disconnected from the electric current activating her body and mind. Only her belly stirred as if it had some external source of power, a generator operating solely for its benefit.

And so the days passed, from the end of 1973 to the beginning of 1974. Yonit went on staying in Benhazar's parents' apartment, doing only what was strictly necessary and hardly ever going out – afraid he might call, give some sign of life precisely when she wasn't there.

As her body grew heavier, her fair hair dulled and grayed, her face grew doughy. Black rings encircled her eyes. Her belly showed signs less of the creation of new life than of rapid and premature aging. Visits from family and friends grew less and less frequent. The soldiers from Benhazar's unit remained in the south, and she rarely saw them. Her department at the university began to train two new doctoral candidates. Her parents sank into depression with her. She sensed their looks, reproaching her for getting involved so lightheartedly in this ill-considered "adventure."

Only to the thread connecting her to Leonardo and Sarina did Yonit cling with all her strength. In their presence she felt that she was close to Benhazar. Leonardo's devotion to her knew no bounds. For hours she would sit and talk with him and Sarina, and when words failed them they would sit and stare with an absentminded air at the old-fashioned black telephone on Benhazar's desk. Again and again they urged her to come and stay with them in their spacious home, but she was adamant in her refusal. As much as she had previously disliked the apartment which in her eyes symbolized the historical baggage from which she sought to detach the friend who had become her husband, she now clung to it as a key link in the invisible chain connecting her to Benhazar.

Every now and then she visited Irena. In some strange, miraculous way her mother-in-law's unique, unpredictable world had become an increasingly powerful ray of light in her darkness. Benhazar's disappearance was not a mystery in the eyes of his mother. On the contrary, to her it seemed a natural and welcome development – as if after long planning and with a specific purpose in mind, he had traveled to some destination beyond the sea.

"Jochanan went up in smoke," she would repeat, "and Kalamaro evaporated as well. Don't worry, my dove, they are both here and there, in the great spaces. Benhazar is connected to them, he set out after them."

In her most difficult hours, in the long sleepless nights, Yonit grew more and more convinced that Irena was right. She thought of Sarina's Chinese boy, of the distant Hong Kong she had never seen, of the endless spaces personified for her by the picture of the Gobi Desert hanging in Leonardo's and Sarina's apartment, and the more she thought of Benhazar's life, the better she understood that her meeting with him was nothing but a miraculous crossroads, and that Benhazar had to continue his journey from there onwards. She reconstructed his actions and words on the eve of the "great party," and she understood that everything was planned in advance, that Irena was right. Her pregnancy and the child in her womb too were a part of what she began to call to herself "the plan."

The war had taken everybody by surprise, but had it really come as a surprise to him? Perhaps it had simply fitted in with his secret plans and made it even easier for him to realize his intentions and confirmed for him the feeling that he was doing the right thing? It was true, she admitted to herself in moments of sober clarity, that it all sounded crazy, illogical, but there were some things that had more to them than met the eye.

She hid these thoughts from her relatives and well-wishers, and opened her heart only to Irena in her hospital room. Irena's long silences too, grew shorter. Now that they had a common subject, their talk flowed like a never-ending stream. So eloquent were these conversations, so logical did Irena's words sound to her, that Yonit decided there was no point in leaving her in the hospital any longer: she would take her home with her and look after all her needs. One day she revealed this plan to Dr. Schechter, when she bumped into him in one of the dark hospital hallways. The doctor stood still, looked at her with his compassionate eyes, and like a concerned father urged her to stop visiting Mrs. Cohen so often.

"You must think of the baby," he said and dropped his eyes to her belly.

Yonit dismissed his advice with scorn, and her visits to Irena grew both longer and more frequent.

In the following weeks and months, while the news on the radio could hardly keep up with the dramatic events in the wake of the war, the ties between Yonit and the hospital inmates grew closer. To them she was a kind of "angel" – an intelligent and reliable contact with the outside world. When she passed through the iron gates Levy the gatekeeper hurried to welcome her, and then shook his head and mumbled to himself, "Poor thing, poor thing." And in order to calm his agitated spirits he would down a little glass of arrack and then increase the volume of the old radio and immerse himself in sad and distant songs.

One day in February 1974, when most of the reserve soldiers were still drafted, Yonit received a visit from Uri, the second in command of the battalion, a sturdy farmer from a moshav. He was wearing dusty fatigues and carrying a backpack and a gun. When he came in she saw the steel helmet hanging behind his shoulder. It was clear that he had come specially to tell her details that had been kept secret from her up to then. Yonit led him into the living room, and after he hesitantly took a seat, she hurried to the kitchen and brought a jug of juice and some baked goods which she took straight out of the fridge without bothering to heat them. Uri looked at her and her enormous belly, the expression on his face changed, and from his tone she understood that he had given up his original intention: he would not tell her what he had come to tell her.

Yonit looked straight into his eyes and tried to compel him to disclose what was on his mind, and Uri tried to avoid her eyes, but failed. Try as he might to divert the conversation into small talk, his thoughts kept returning to the astonishing information he had come to impart. For a while he went on vacillating, wiping the sweat off his forehead, and in the end, when he realized that she was stronger than he was, and that she was determined to hear what he had to tell, he told her, as if confessing, about the special relationship that had grown up between himself and Benhazar during the war, and even before it, during their stints of service in the reserves.

"For hours on end we would talk," he said. "The radio would beep and we would pay no attention and go on talking our heads off until dawn. Once I even relieved one of the soldiers of guard duty and sent him off to sleep so that I could talk to Benhazar without anyone to disturb us. We went on patrols together day and night. He was ready for any duty. When I told him to go and get some sleep or take a rest he would refuse. 'Sleep is an escape,' he said. Strange, but in spite of the deep bond formed between us, I didn't really understand him. He formulated his ideas in a complex, original way, and they didn't fit into any accepted political framework.

"Benhazar was angry about the war. He blamed Golda, Dayan, and their close political associates and friends not only for the technical failure, but also for the terrible political failure that had begun in 1967. There were moments when I thought that he didn't even want us to win, and nevertheless he volunteered for every mission and was never deterred by any danger. He was an asset to the battalion. And everyone close to him knew it. 'Only a draw and the restoration of the Arab nation's lost honor,' he would say, 'will bring peace.' He didn't sound like a member of our own generation. The examples he quoted were remote, even harking back to the British Mandate.

For him all of history and politics were one. He jumped from Kissinger to Churchill, from Lechi to the Haganah; he made connections between events and personalities I knew nothing about: Burma, the Sino-Japanese war, Marshal Pétain and Wang Ching-wei. I'm sorry, perhaps I didn't understand, perhaps I'm doing him an injustice."

Uri fell silent and looked at Yonit like a scolded boy. It was obvious that he was not satisfied with the way he had presented his case. He waved his hand in a brief, dismissive gesture, as if to wipe out everything he had said, and smiled sadly. Yonit giggled. She recognized Benhazar's words in what Uri had just said, but in a jumbled, fragmented and distorted fashion.

"Didn't he ever mention his father Jochanan?" she whispered.

"Yes, once," replied Uri. "We were lying in a shallow trench and there was a hellish bombardment going on around us. Then a ghastly silence fell. Not even the wounded cried out. In his heart of hearts every one of us thanked God that he had come out of it in one piece. Benhazar was the first to speak.

"'After the war,' he said, 'I'll go and visit my father. I wonder what he'll say now?'"

"Did he tell you where his father was?"

"No. For some reason I thought he was working abroad, in Asia apparently."

Yonit said nothing. A tremor ran through her body. For a moment the figure of Irena appeared before her. She lowered her eyes and then abruptly raised her head.

"Go on, Uri. I know you have news."

"No, no," Uri stammered and drew back in his chair. "I'm sorry to say I have no news. From time to time investigation teams come to the battalion, they question me, the company commander, the platoon commander, the soldiers who were with Benhazar. They try to reconstruct the movements of the platoon, to uncover new facts, but up to now they haven't discovered anything."

"So what else have you got to tell me?" demanded Yonit.

"Nothing, Yonit, really, nothing. A couple of times I assembled Behhazar's company. I explained to them that every scrap of information possessed by any of them about his movements before he disappeared, and especially on the day of his disappearance, was vitally important, that anyone who remembered anything should come to me at once, day or night."

"Look, Uri," said Yonit, "you have nothing to fear. I'm in the sixth month, and nothing will happen to the baby," she patted her belly gently. "He's the only hope remaining to me. Please tell me."

Uri took a cigarette out of his shirt pocket and lit it, and Yonit saw that it was the only one there, without a packet, as if it had found its way into his pocket by mistake. The movements of Uri's hands and the smoke spiralling up to the ceiling seemed to announce the change that had taken place in him. Yonit tensed, and he suddenly said: "Something strange happened. You know that the battalion is still deployed in the area of the bridges over the canal, between the Egyptian Second Army in the north and the Third Army in the south. There's a constant fear that the two armies will close in on us and cut off our forces on the other side of the canal. We have a platoon in the 'Chinese Farm' opposite the troops of the Second Army. It's a slaughterhouse, like nothing we've ever seen here before. Smashed and burnt steel, human and machine parts, as if some giant monster ran amok in a children's nursery and smashed the lead soldiers and the little play weapons to smithereens.

"Yes, you wouldn't believe it, but there are huge tanks there, terrifying hulks of steel, standing twisted like pieces of plastic exposed to an open fire. Scores of vehicles, ours and the enemy's. The fields are mined. Even today you have to move cautiously there. There are marked squares that are out of bounds, where entry is forbidden by order. From time to time the C.O. and I go on tours of inspection between the various platoons, and God help anyone caught disobeying orders and wandering among the burned-out tanks, looking for booty, enemy binoculars, telescopes, and the rest of the 'souvenirs', as the soldiers call the items they pick up and push deep into their backpacks.

"This kind of disobedience can be paid for with the loss of an arm or a leg. The whole area is strewn with the remains of cluster bombs – cute little balls that can blow up at any minute. Mines, shells and all kinds of explosives are lying around just waiting to be activated. But nevertheless I regret to say that there are still booty hunters who insist on going out there and we've already had three men wounded. After they recover they'll be court martialed. When someone's moving around the area, even on a partisan illegal expedition, there's always a man in his platoon who knows where he is; they simply cover up for each other. They set up lookouts to warn them if our jeep's approaching the area to catch the culprits and put them on trial.

"And just lately, on two separate occasions, I was told by two soldiers stationed quite a distance from each other that they had seen a mysterious figure wandering around the area. They claimed that it was neither an Egyptian soldier nor one of ours.

When I asked how such a thing was possible, they admitted that it was illogical, that it didn't make sense, and nevertheless, they said, it was a fact. At first I didn't attach any importance to it and I sent them both away with a joke: even ghosts and devils wouldn't dare move around in such a dangerous place, I said. But the more I thought about it, the more it seemed to me that there was something weird going on here, and I spoke to the commander of the 'Chinese Farm' platoon and asked him, without giving him any explanations, to keep an eye on his soldiers and check if there were any 'foreign elements' (those were my very words) moving around in the area. Until three days ago I didn't hear anything and I forgot about the whole affair.

"But at the end of last week, after a visit to the 'Farm,' I was approached by a nebbish-looking, bespectacled soldier who said simply, 'Listen, Uri, Benhazar's wandering round the minefields here!!' I was shocked out of my mind. What can I tell you? I broke out in a cold sweat. I've already been in all kinds of difficult situations in my life, but facing something like this, something supernatural, I was helpless. After a minute I recovered, grabbed four-eyes by the collar and shook him as if he were to blame for Benhazar's disappearance, for the outbreak of the war, for everything. I shook him again and again and tried to get the whole truth out of him. He was afraid I was going to strangle him and he yelled: 'You're killing me, what do you want?' But I couldn't stop. I yelled at him like a madman: 'Show me exactly where you saw him, why didn't you report it at once, why didn't you arrest him?' But the poor devil couldn't answer me. In the end I calmed down, sat on the ground and pulled him down by his collar after me. Then I let go of him and said, 'OK, now talk quietly.' He told me that he'd seen Benhazar once. That morning he'd gone off a little way from the platoon posts in order to relieve himself and he arrived at a point from which he could see an area invisible to anyone manning the extreme post. In the middle of this area, which was usually out of bounds, next to a couple of Egyptian tanks, he saw Benhazar dressed in a light khaki uniform with a broad-brimmed IDF hat on his head."

Uri's voice trembled. Again he looked into Yonit's face with a hesitant, apologetic expression, and for a moment he seemed about to stop, but she indicated with a calm nod of her head that he should continue. Suddenly he was amazed at her composure, at the inexplicable serenity with which she greeted his words. Could it be that she wasn't surprised?

"I haven't got much more to add," he said after a brief pause. "The soldier was prepared to swear that it was Benhazar, but before he could decide what to do, the figure had already disappeared. The soldier didn't tell anyone what he had seen – he was afraid they would laugh at him. He persuaded himself that it was his imagination, a mirage, but the figure of Benhazar haunted him, and he decided to tell me. 'I've been suffering from terrible migraines lately,' he admitted, 'but nevertheless, between us, I truly believe that I saw Benhazar.'"

"What else?" asked Yonit dryly.

"Nothing. I told the platoon commander to set up ambushes on the borders of the platoon territory. I told him that there were intelligence reports of some mysterious figure wandering around in the area, but I didn't give him any details."

The month of February drew to a close, and March and April too passed. Yonit received another official letter from the army Manpower and Personnel Administration, but she refused to accept what it said. She had long ago stopped paying any attention to what was told her by official representatives of the army, chaplains, and other well-intentioned people.

On the fourteenth of May Jonathan was born.

One Saturday in the middle of summer she went as usual to the hospital at the bottom of Disraeli Street, carrying Jonathan next to her chest. When she went into Irena's room she found her lying on her bed, uncharacteristically silent, at her side an illustrated weekly that Benhazar had sometimes read. Then she handed the weekly to Yonit and pointed to a boxed item on one of the inside pages.

Under the headline "Now It Can Be Disclosed," a well-known military correspondent reported that in the course of a tour in the area of the canal bridges he had conducted in February, he had interviewed reservists from an anti-aircraft unit about their political opinions. "After talking to them, when I was about to climb onto the jeep," the correspondent wrote, "four of the soldiers offered to share their battle rations with me and talk about the situation informally and off the record. I was happy to accept their invitation.

"'There was one thing in this war,' they told me, 'that came as a pleasant surprise – the information policy of the chief education officer. There's an openness, you could even say a fresh breeze of original, controversial ideas blowing. Just a week ago,' the kibbutznik in the group offered by way of example, 'a young information officer came to our unit, without insignia, a little weird, wearing a nonstandard light khaki uniform and an IDF hat on his head. He held forth eloquently and enthusiastically about his opinions. The main theme of his lecture was the need for a draw, for a delicate balance between us and the Arabs. This war, he promised, would lead to peace, not because our victory this time was absolute, but precisely because our success was limited and didn't humiliate our enemies. A crushing military victory, he argued fervently, is not a guarantee of political success, just as losing a local battle need not necessarily mean losing the war. Up to now we've been strong, too strong, and therefore also too proud. Between arrogance and humiliation there can never be peace. This is a new tune and we're expecting things to change.'"

With this familiar quotation the reporter concluded his article.